THE
ICE PICK
ARTIST

Also by Harold Adams

The Man Who Was Taller Than God
A Perfectly Proper Murder
A Way With Widows
The Ditched Blonde
Hatchet Job

THE
ICE PICK
ARTIST

A Carl Wilcox Mystery

HAROLD ADAMS

Harold Adams

WALKER AND COMPANY
NEW YORK

Copyright © 1997 by Harold Adams

First published in the United States of America in 1997 by
Walker Publishing Company, Inc.

Published simultaneously in Canada by Thomas Allen & Son Canada,
Limited, Markham, Ontario

Library of Congress Cataloging-in-Publication Data
Adams, Harold, 1923-
The ice pick artist: a Carl Wilcox mystery/Harold Adams.
p. cm.
ISBN 0-8027-3310-7
I. Title.
PS3551.D367I28   1997
813' .54—dc21   97-23563
CIP

Printed in the United States of America
2 4 6 8 10 9 7 5 3 1

To Bill Malloy and Michael Seidman,
two editors who have given me great
professional support and
encouragement for many years.

THE
ICE PICK
ARTIST

1

IN THE FALL that year I gave up sign-painting travels and went back to Corden. My nephew Hank was off to college in Brookings; my old man, Elihu, spent his days in bed or a wheelchair; and business was too lousy to hire anybody competent, so of course the hobo son had to come home and hold off the wolf from the door.

I figured at least the chow would be good, but on the first day it became clear Elihu's troubles distracted Bertha, our cook, so bad she was tolerating Ma in her kitchen. To put it kindly, the menu suffered.

To top things off, just about supper time on a Sunday, this woman arrived. She was small and round where it counts, with slim ankles, great calves, and powerful thighs. I watched her slip out of her new Oldsmobile and walk up to the door wearing a dark topcoat, a dinky hat, and an expression somewhere between pained and resigned as she took in the Wilcox Hotel.

"Do you have bedbugs?" she demanded as we faced each other over the check-in counter.

2 / H A R O L D A D A M S

"No ma'am. Anything that can't pay, can't stay."

She looked startled, then grinned, and I knew this was a chubby one I could go for.

"The last hotel I stayed in had them by the millions. It made me leery."

"If it made you anemic, it sure doesn't show. You want a room?"

"Got one with running water? And don't tell me only when it rains."

"I won't, and we do. Number ten. Best room in the house. The bed's got an innerspring mattress, there's a new sink, and you can even get hot water if you're willing to pay. The bathroom's just a hop, skip, and a jump down the hall."

She sighed and, with a bold hand that fit her style, wrote down Lilybell Fox, from Sioux Falls, South Dakota.

Ordinarily I don't haul luggage, since guests in our hotel run 99 percent male, ugly, or both. When this one asked for help I hopped. The only luggage I'd handled that was heavier than hers was the sea chest of a mad sailor who stopped by the first year my old man opened the hotel. He was the reason I normally turned down helping guests. Lilybell about finished off all my chivalrous inclinations

"You're strong," she told me when I set the cases on the floor in her room. "Most men can't carry more than one of those at a time."

"I've got more muscles than brains," I confessed, "but if you don't unload the bricks in these before you leave, I'll just drop the cases off the balcony when you check out."

"Well," she said, handing me a quarter, "at least you won't worry about me sneaking out early in the morning without paying, right?"

"About the hot water," she said as I pocketed the tip and started out. "I'll want it by eight in the morning."

"That's another two bits."

"Put it on my bill. Does this place have a dining room?"

"Yup, but it's not open anymore. You'll find a place east half a block on the south side. They haven't poisoned anybody in years."

Fifteen minutes later she came down the stairs, gave me an airy wave, went into the cool fall evening, and headed east. I watched her ankles and neat swaying walk until she was out of sight.

A gloomy dude in a dark gray suit showed up ten minutes later, asked for a room, and signed in. His writing was so lousy I couldn't make out the name. I asked how he pronounced it.

"Murdoff," he growled. He had eyebrows you could trim with hedge clippers, a furrowed brow, big ears, and a spade-shaped jaw. Made me think of Karloff doing Frankenstein's monster with a constipation bellyache. He smelled of menthol, and I guessed he was sucking a cough drop.

"Is that Hopkins, Minnesota, you're from?" I asked, staring at the address.

His dark eyes bored into me.

"That's right. You got any more questions?"

"Yeah, how long are you staying?"

"The night."

He didn't glance my way when he came back down from the room, just tramped through the front door and headed east on Main. I went out and looked at his black Packard. It wasn't new or clean, and the tires had lots of experience. The license plate was a South Dakota job with numbers showing it came from Sioux Falls.

I'd been back in the lobby about five minutes when Ma came in from her parlor and, as usual, drifted over to squint at who'd signed in. She had as much trouble with Murdoff's scribbling as I did, but suddenly brightened at the sight of the signature above.

"Lilybell—my land, I've not seen that name in ages. What's she look like?"

"Mata Hari," I said, straight-faced. "Real vamp."

She said, "Hah!" looked at the new guest addresses, and walked over to stare at the cars out front.

"Hers is the Olds," I said. "His the Packard."

"How interesting. Both with Sioux Falls plates, but he claims to be from Minnesota. They come in together?"

"About ten minutes apart."

She checked the room numbers and asked if both guests were upstairs.

"Nope. Both went out, heading east. Probably smooching in a booth at the café."

She thought about that, moved over to the rocker nearest the check-in counter, and sat down.

"Why don't you go see?"

I gave her my owliest look. "Why?"

"Because we'd both like to know."

It seemed likely I'd find Lilybell in a booth and the Halloween haunt at the counter, but it turned out the opposite. She was parked at the last stool near the kitchen, jawing with Eric, the owner. Actually she wasn't jawing, he was. She had him wound up like a music box. Old Murdoff was working on a hot beef sandwich as if it were the only thing in the world important.

I slipped onto a stool near mid-counter, and Rose came over, smiling.

"Need a cherry pie à la mode," I told her.

"I guess Bertha's not back to cooking regular," she said. Rose always understood. She delivered my order, and I enjoyed it with coffee and wondered why I'd never married this woman. Maybe because she seemed to have jinxed so many guys. She saw me sneaking peeks to my left and gave me a wise grin.

"You like that?"

I shrugged.

"You like them all," she said. "That's your whole trouble."

I didn't think it was my *whole* trouble, but it came close enough that it didn't seem worth arguing.

"You talk any with old Frankenstein over there in the booth?" I asked.

She shook her head and shuddered.

"What's the matter?"

"He's evil," she whispered.

"How'd you figure that—just because he looks like a haunt?"

"The way he glared at the lady when he came in. He looked murder at her."

"Say anything?"

"No. Just took the booth and hasn't looked her way since."

"She look at him?"

"She doesn't know he exists, far as I can tell."

2

I DRANK COFFEE after finishing my pie and ice cream, and saw Lilybell tip her head my way and ask Eric a question. He grinned and leaned close to talk lower.

A few moments later she got up and strolled my way, heading for the checkout up front as Eric walked behind the counter parallel with her. She paused by me.

"Mind taking me for a walk and showing off your town?"

"Think you can stand the excitement?"

"I'll steel myself to it."

I tried to catch whether she glanced toward Murdoff as we headed out, but she didn't turn her head, so I couldn't tell.

Outside we ambled west. The wind had fallen off with the setting sun, and what was left felt cool. She raised her collar and pulled the little hat tight over her brown curls.

"So, what'd Eric tell you about Corden?" I asked.

"He thinks it's the flower of the prairie and has nothing but sterling characters living in it. He hinted that perhaps you were the only doubtful one in the batch."

"What'd he say about me?"

"That you have a terrible reputation for woman chasing, fight a lot, and have even been in prison. The weirdest thing is, he also claims you've worked as a policeman. I thought it was only in the old Wild West where outlaws became lawmen."

"There are all kinds of cops."

"I'm sure. Eric says you've been trapped by the hotel since your father's stroke."

"How come you're poking into all of this?"

"Because I'm curious. Like you. And don't tell me you didn't trail me to the café to find out what I'd be up to."

"Okay, what are you doing in town?"

"Looking for a garden spot to settle down and live in tranquillity."

"You don't seem the type."

"What type do you take me for?"

"A woman who knows what she wants, and it's got nothing to do with—what'd you call it? Tranquillity?"

She laughed and tilted her head as she looked at me. "What gives you that idea, my mink coat and all the diamonds?"

"It's in the eyes and the style. You're not the retiring kind."

We stopped at the corner, and she turned to study me for several seconds. "How come you look like a loser and talk like a mensch?"

"What the hell's a mensch?"

She laughed again. "It's normally a man who wouldn't have to ask that question. Now come on, don't get sore—I'm sure you're not really a loser, but you do look tough. That's fine, I'm not the kind that's impressed by pretty boys."

We walked north and east to the park and softball diamonds. The elms and box elders were still hanging on the green leaves well after the cottonwoods had turned gold and shed bare. The air smelled of fall, and the grass looked dead.

We stood a moment, looking across the ball fields.

"Where are the better homes?" she asked.

"There are some a block southwest, more up on the west hill and on the south end. Who're you looking for?"

"I'm not sure. Somebody interesting, special. Let's try the west hill."

We started up the long, easy slope. As we passed houses, she asked who lived in each and what they did for a living. I was surprised by how many I couldn't name. The fact is, even in a dinky place like Corden, you can't know everybody, it just seems you do.

A Model A Ford purred past, turned left at the first corner, and was gone.

Few houses stand out in Corden; some are just bigger than others and better kept up, with neater lawns and newer sidewalks. The one she stopped me at was the Tobiason place. He was the area photographer, doing weddings, graduation portraits, and special events. Lilybell stared at the three-story house, which stood on a slope about six feet above the sidewalk. Two big evergreens flanking the walk hid much of the front.

"Who lives here?" she asked.

I told her.

"A photographer? In Corden?"

"That's right. He does okay. Out back there's a studio with a big skylight."

"That's amazing."

"It doesn't hurt that his father-in-law had money and left his daughter the house and some left over."

"What was his name?"

"Colonel Cameron Cutter. One of the founders of Corden County, along with his brother, Vic."

"Where'd their money come from?"

I shrugged. Not being an ancient history nut, I'd never been that interested.

She didn't ask any more questions, and after a moment we moved on.

Down the west hill we turned south, crossing the railroad tracks a few yards beyond the hotel. She spotted Boswell's shack over half a block west near the tracks, and asked me who lived there.

I told her his name and that he'd been the town's moonshiner during Prohibition.

"What's he do now?"

"Mostly smokes a pipe, naps, and remembers."

"He must go back to the town's beginnings."

"About as early as the railroad. Eighteen eighty-five, I think."

"Would he talk with me?"

"Boswell'd talk with visiting mice and stray flies."

"Good," she said, and headed for the shack.

"Was his place made from boxcar sidings?" she asked as we approached the front.

"That's right. You can see the windows are catty-wampus. That's because Boswell was squiffed when he put them in."

I squinted inside and tapped on the screen door edge. Boswell's ancient face showed up through the cabin's gloom, first his gray stubble beard, then the bleary eyes, and finally the stained teeth as he grinned his greeting and shoved the screen open.

As usual, he looked as if he'd just got up after sleeping all night in his clothes. His tired eyes opened a little at the sight of Lilybell, but he accepted her as he did most everything in life, with approval. That his single room looked like an untidy corner of a dump didn't faze him a jot, and he waved her toward his battered easy chair, offered me the straight-backed he used at his dinky dining table, and sat down on his rumpled bed.

Lilybell asked when he first came to Corden.

"Eighteen eighty-five."

"Is that when the railroad came through?"

"Nope. That was eighty-three. I started work with 'em in eighty-five."

"You made your home here then?"

"Didn't build this place 'til nineteen twenty-five, when I retired from the railroad and took on janitoring at Corden High. Did that three years."

"And started moonshining in twenty-eight?"

He grinned. "Uh-huh."

"So after Repeal, you retired again?"

"Yup."

She smiled at him cozily.

"I suppose you knew Colonel Cutter?"

"Sure, Old Cameron built a sod house just about where the courthouse stands now. Spent his first year trapping muskrat, mink, and foxes. Lived on deer, antelope, fish, and prairie chickens that first winter. Him and Vic and some others."

"Vic was his brother, wasn't he?"

"Uh-huh. Some older."

Lilybell's eyes glowed as she leaned toward the old man.

"Did you know Victor's wife?"

"Mattie? Sure thing."

"They had children, didn't they?"

"Yup. Iva, a little girl, and a boy, Wayne."

"And they became wards of the colonel, right?"

"Seems like."

"How did it happen they got turned over to the uncle, when Mattie Cutter was capable of handling the sale of Vic's property?"

Boswell frowned and finally shook his head. "I don't know she handled that. Seems more like it was the colonel. He handled about everything for everybody, seems like. But I don't recollect that too good."

"Do you know why Victor went out in that blizzard?"

"Mattie said he insisted on going to the well for water and must've got lost. Maybe had a heart attack or something. After the storm, they found him out west of the barn, buried in snow and frozen stiff."

Lilybell nodded thoughtfully, and after a little more polite talk, we left.

3

"WHY," I ASKED as we walked back toward the hotel, "are you poking into the history of the Cutter clan?"

She gave me a cozy smile.

"One of my closest friends is Iva, the colonel's niece. When she was very young, her mother gave up her brother and her to their uncle. She's never understood why, and it's always haunted her. Since I was recently widowed and my husband left me enough to get by on, I decided it might be interesting to dig into the whole business."

"Why didn't you say so in the first place?"

"I didn't want to come stomping in, stirring up old rumors, and maybe getting people's backs up. It seemed sensible to feel things out a little first. Besides, I thought it'd be more fun to see what I could pick up by indirection. What's wrong with that?"

"It seems damned roundabout."

"Well, it might, to a man. Guys always have to barge straight ahead. That's boring. That was my husband's style. I'm not stuck with it anymore, and I plan to make the most of that."

"Your husband bored you, huh?"

"Oh Lord, yes. Not just with directness—sometimes that's fine, but he carried it to extremes. Besides that, he had a million other foibles."

"Like asking 'What's a foible?' "

She glanced at me suspiciously, then grinned.

"He never had the guts to admit he didn't know a word I used. You're not like that, are you? No phony. Okay, let's get down to cases, directly. You've been very nice to show me around and answer all my questions. So what do you think is in this for you?"

"Anything from a few laughs to a snuggle-up."

"Really? Am I supposed to be flattered that you're interested in me personally? You think I'm a loose woman?"

"More like an independent one. Ordinary ones don't travel alone in this territory. I figure you make your own rules."

"Well, aren't you clever to guess I'd like that approach? But what you're really after is, what am I up to? Right?"

"That's part of it."

"Uh-huh. A little learning and maybe another score. Well, who knows?"

Ma was knitting in the rocker nearest the register when we entered the lobby, and after greeting her, Lilybell went upstairs. I settled in Elihu's swivel chair by the window overlooking town.

"Did Murdoff come back?"

"No. What have you learned about Mrs. Fox?"

I told her, leaving out the little chatter on the way back from the café. I'd just finished when Lilybell came back down, strolled across the lobby, and after a glance at the papers on the big table under the clock, took a rocker next to Gabriel's bird cage and smiled at us brightly.

"Is your family the one that was involved with Colonel Cutter?" asked Ma.

"I'm just an in-law of the clan. But I'm a good friend of Iva, the colonel's niece."

"Oh yes, I remember Iva. A pretty little thing, but awfully shy. Did she ever grow out of that?"

"Well, she's still pretty, but not little, and certainly far from shy. Do you happen to know why she and Wayne were turned over to the colonel when Victor died?"

"I always presumed it was because Mattie couldn't care for them alone. Why, do you think there was something more to it?"

"Iva does. She claims all the Cutter family avoided talk of her father's death, and she never saw her mother again as a child after she was separated from her about a week following the blizzard. That's when the children were officially made wards of the colonel. As far as Iva knows, no one ever questioned why Mattie wasn't considered competent to care for her own daughter and son."

"Well," said Ma, "I remember a few stories. Like, the colonel wanted the children because he and his wife had none and Mattie preferred to pass the children on to someone who could provide for them better than she could. It can be very difficult for a widow with two children in this territory."

"Was there suspicion about how Vic croaked?" I asked.

Both women looked at me, Ma shocked, Lilybell just thoughtful.

"What were the stories about that?" I asked.

Lilybell shifted in her chair and settled back.

"The one I heard was that when Victor went out with his water pail, Mattie was supposed to stand by the door and bang on a pan to guide him back to the house if he had trouble finding his way in the blinding blizzard. But later, when some busybody talked with the kids, neither of them remembered hearing that pan being banged. In fact, little Wayne thought his mother never stepped close to the door, open or closed.

Most adults didn't pay that any mind, figuring that under the circumstances the kids were too young to understand what was going on."

"I thought farmers around here in those days always ran an overhead line from the back door to the well as a guide during whiteouts."

Lilybell shrugged. "If they had one, it went down somehow."

"How old were the kids then?"

"Wayne was about four and a half, Iva was six."

"Did Victor knock around his wife or the kids?"

"Not according to Iva. He was bossy, arbitrary, and domineering, but that's how men are."

That got an agreeing nod from Ma, who had just heard herself described to a T.

I asked Lilybell whether she knew if Mattie had tried to fight for her kids.

"I asked Iva that. She said she didn't think so, but of course she was so young at the time she probably wouldn't know. It doesn't seem, from anything Iva said about her, that Mattie was exactly a doting mother."

After a few moments of silence, I asked Lilybell if she knew anything about a man named Murdoff. She said no.

"The waitress at the café says he looked daggers at you when he came in there tonight, while you were chatting up Eric. Didn't you notice him come in?"

"The tall man, with the cadaver face? I saw him, but he didn't interest me, so I paid no attention."

"It seems awfully funny, two people from Sioux Falls showing up in Corden within fifteen minutes of each other, at this hotel. Seems like a pretty far-fetched coincidence."

She shrugged nonchalantly. "Strange things happen all the time. He tell you how long he was staying?"

"Just the night."

"Well, tomorrow he'll be gone—while I stay on."

Soon after that she went up to her room.

Murdoff showed up about half an hour later, after Ma had gone to bed. He checked the wall clock against his pocket watch, gave me a baleful look, and went upstairs.

Glancing at the register before going to bed, I noticed a new name under Murdoff's—James Olson, of Fargo, North Dakota. A check mark on the line indicated that he'd paid in advance, and he'd left no call.

I headed for my room, thinking that James Olson was about like John Smith in our territory. That would account for his payment in advance, which Ma had probably insisted on, especially if he were traveling light.

IN THE MORNING I turned on the water heater just after seven-thirty, and at eight, I went to room ten and knocked.

No answer. A harder knock got the same result. I turned the knob and pushed the door open. Sun penetrated the drawn shades, giving the room a warm golden glow and lighting up the bed clearly. Lilybell was on her back, under the covers, with the sheet over her face and her right arm dangling over the bed's edge.

It didn't take an autopsy to tell me she was dead.

I went to Murdoff's door and pounded. No reaction except an angry mutter from a neighboring room. It was no surprise to find, on entering, that the bed was empty and his suitcase gone.

4

CORDEN'S COP, JOEY, stared gloomily at the murdered woman as Doc Feeney gently pulled the sheet back over the still body on the best mattress in the Wilcox Hotel.

"I'd guess it was an ice pick," said Doc. "Right between the ribs. Three times."

"Jesus," said Joey reverently.

"The killer probably held the pillow over her face when he struck. Keep her from screaming."

"When?" asked Joey.

"Sometime last night," said Doc.

Doc's sarcasm always gave Joey the look of a man with gas pains.

"Get her over to my office," Doc told me. "I'll have to do it right."

We got a stretcher from city hall and made the delivery. It reminded me of carrying Flory Fancett's body, a few years back, to the same office with a deputy's help. Only that time I was the prime suspect. It didn't give me any relief to know this time nobody'd be accusing Carl Wilcox—I was too much involved in thinking how the hell to nail the ice pick artist who'd done the job on Lilybell.

"You get the license number of that guy Murdoff?" Joey asked.

"Nothing but the 1A for Sioux Falls."

After leaving Lilybell with Doc, we went back to the hotel and examined Murdoff's registration again. All that did was confirm his lousy penmanship.

Joey stared at me gloomily.

"All right. You went to Murdoff's room after you found the girl's body. He'd skipped, right?"

"Right."

"You check the room of this Olson guy?"

I had. It was empty too.

We talked with Ma. The murder hadn't scared her, it just fired up indignation and sharpened her memory, which was all too good any time. She said Olson was a very young man who showed up half an hour after I'd left for Eric's Café. He carried only a small bag and paid in advance, saying he'd be leaving early in the morning and didn't need a call. He was about average height, wore a gray cap and a trench coat with the collar up. His nose was long and narrow, with wide nostrils; he had heavy eyebrows. He walked with a rolling gait, like he might be bowlegged. She thought he met her eyes a little too directly, as though he were trying to seem open and at the same time wanted to bully her. Of course, if he'd avoided her eyes she absolutely would have spotted him for a crook. With Ma, moderation is everything.

I gave Joey a description of Murdoff's kisser and the make of his car. He made scribbling notes and ambled mournfully back to his office to see what he could do on the telephone.

Ma and I had a kitchen conference, trying to work out which Cutter and Fox family members we might contact. That went nowhere, so I decided to go see Boswell again.

He was sitting by the front door in his straight-backed chair, tilted against the shack's outside wall while he sucked on his stubby pipe and swigged coffee from a fat mug.

My report on Lilybell changed his normally peaceful face to something like a sad clown's mask. He lowered the front chair legs to the ground, set aside the pipe and mug, and got out his red bandanna to mop his moist cheeks. It was an ungodly shame, he said; she'd seemed such a lively girl, bright and fine.

"You going to find who done it?" he asked.

"I'll sure try. Where's her friend Iva live now?"

"Aberdeen. Married to a fella named Johanson who runs a hardware store—Johanson's."

"Know anything about him?"

He shook his head, retrieved his pipe, knocked the dottle out, and wished me luck.

Back at the hotel Ma looked up at me from the rocker nearest the registration counter. She'd been talking with Margaret, she said, the grass widow who came to help Bertha the time Elihu had his first stroke and he and Ma went to California during South Dakota's pheasant-hunting season. "She's willing to come back and help if you have to be gone awhile," she added.

There wasn't much point in asking why she thought I'd be traveling. I told her what Boswell had to offer, then went over to city hall and located Joey in his cubbyhole office. He nodded gloomily over my report and agreed it'd be good if I'd make the trip and dig around. He couldn't guarantee any pay for my travel expenses, since the lady killed wasn't from Corden, and the city fathers weren't likely to figure chasing the killer was a big item for the county. It didn't do any good to point out what damage an unsolved murder could do to our tourist business— we never did have any except hunters, who are hard to scare since they all bring guns when they come to stay.

The trip to Aberdeen took about two hours of whizzing along at forty miles per, with fine views of dusty roads, burned grain fields, tumbleweeds, and bony livestock. I even saw a few cars and a couple trucks along the way, and passed through towns smaller and scruffier than Corden.

Johanson's Hardware was bigger than Gambles in Corden, and I found it on my first sashay down the main drag. I don't know that hardware stores have their own scent, but something about them always gives me a little lift. Groceries do the same thing. Maybe because in small towns these stores supply nearly all the necessities and sell the least junk.

A young guy in a carpenter's apron greeted me, and I asked him for the boss before he could offer help. He said he was in the back room and went to get him.

Johanson was a lanky dude with thick-lensed, wire-frame glasses that made his eyeballs owlish. A shock of wild, dark hair, salted with gray, flopped across his high forehead. His expression let me know he would never expect anything good from a stranger with a broken nose.

"You know a woman named Lilybell?" I asked.

"Yes?"

"Good friend of your wife's, right?"

"She's close to both of us. Why are you asking?"

"I'm sorry, I've got bad news. You know she was visiting in Corden this week?"

"Seems Iva said something about it, yeah. What's the bad news?"

"She died last night."

His eyebrows arched, and his wide mouth dropped open for a second. Then he swallowed, making his lumpy Adam's apple bounce, and asked what from.

"Somebody put a pillow over her face in room ten of the Wilcox Hotel and stabbed her to death with an ice pick."

"Oh my God—who?"

"Probably a guy who signed in as Murdoff. He came to the hotel right behind her, left in the night without checking out. Name mean anything to you?"

He was so rattled he took a second before shaking his head, and finally asked what the man looked like.

"Something between Frankenstein's monster and an undertaker with TB."

He didn't find that description any help, so I went into a little more detail, without better success. He'd never seen such a man, and the name meant nothing.

"Okay. Maybe your wife can give me some help. What's your home address?"

He scowled and asked just exactly what I had to do with this murder. I explained I was the leg man for Corden's cop, trying to get a lead on why anybody would want to kill Lilybell and make any connections possible with her friends to see if they could help run down the killer.

Johanson dithered a while before giving me the address. He said he'd call and tell Iva what happened, and it would be best if I'd skip any gruesome details because she was very sensitive and would go all to pieces if I upset her.

Mrs. Johanson was standing behind her screen door, watching as I parked in front and came up the walk. She was tall and slim. Long, dark hair parted in the middle framed her face, making it extra pale and narrow. Her dark brown eyes were big and accusing.

She said, "Mr. Wilcox?" and when I nodded, pushed the door open, turned as I took hold of it, and led me into a living room on the left off the entry hall, which had a stairway to the second floor on the right.

She waved me toward the couch, sat on an overstuffed chair next to it, and said, "My husband says you told him Lilybell's been murdered."

"Yeah, I'm sorry. I could tell she thought a lot of you. Guess you were close."

That seemed to offend her. For a second I thought of ditching the details, but decided that'd get me nowhere and told her straight what Lilybell had said about Iva's need to know what happened with her parents.

She shook her head irritably. "I can't imagine her talking like that about me to a stranger. But she was always very sure of herself, and terribly single-minded. When she got an idea in her head, nothing'd do but get to the bottom of it."

"What'd she have in her head?"

"Who knows? She might've given you the notion she was very open and simple, but that wasn't Lilybell in the least. She was a very complicated woman, make no mistake about that. And highly imaginative."

"Why do you think she was in Corden?"

"I don't suppose we'll ever know, now, will we?"

I let that hang and watched her a moment. She stared back, keeping her face stiff.

"Did your husband tell you about the guy from the Cities who showed up at the hotel the night Lilybell came, then disappeared before morning?"

"No. You think he killed her?"

"It seems likely. He was a tall gink with black bushy eyebrows, big ears, and lots of jaw. Probably forty or so. Know anybody like that?"

"Why would I?"

"I figure he might've been one of the Cutter tribe."

"I can't imagine what you're getting at."

"I think somebody didn't want Lilybell poking into the family history. And I think you might know why."

"Oh, come now. Are you suggesting my family history is such that one of them would murder to keep its secrets? What kind of books have you been reading?"

"I'm not a heavy reader, Mrs. Johanson."

"Well, you certainly seem to have a highly overworked imagination."

I grinned at her. She didn't like it, but she said nothing.

"All right," I said. "Let's try another angle. How'd you get to know Lilybell?"

"We were schoolmates in high school, here in Aberdeen. After graduation she moved with her parents to Sioux Falls. We wrote each other, but never got together again until her husband died and she came here to live."

"You never met her husband?"

"No."

"What'd he die of?"

"Heart failure. It was very sudden."

"From what she told me, I got the notion his death didn't exactly break her up. She tell you anything about how things were with them?"

"Well, it was no fairy-tale romance with happy-ever-after. None of them are, are they?"

"She tell you about her husband's family?"

"Some."

"Her husband's family and yours came from the two guys who settled Corden around 1879, right?"

"Yes. Colonel Cutter and Cole Fox. Both served in the Union army during the Civil War and came out here afterward, and their relatives followed them."

"How'd Lilybell like her in-laws?"

"Not a bit."

"Was it mutual?"

"I don't understand you. A minute ago you were suggesting Lilybell was murdered because she was causing family scandals, now you're suggesting the family blamed Lilybell for her husband's death and one of them murdered her for revenge. It seems you're shooting off in all directions."

"What I'm doing is checking all the angles until I find one that fits. If she was your friend, I'd think you'd want to help me out."

For several seconds she just glared, then she took a deep breath and slumped back in her chair.

"All right. You've made your point. Hearing of her death in such an awful way just makes me wild. I can't help being mad, and that's stupid. I'm very sorry. I'll try to help you all I can. Let's just start over."

5

THE FOXES, SAID Iva, were a large family, descendants of one of Aberdeen's original founders, Cole Fox, who earlier on had been a partner of Colonel Cutter in founding Corden. Cole's descendants were too clannish and rowdy for the puritanical majority, who considered them unchristian and common. Everyone assumed Cole and Colonel Cutter were equal partners in the Corden grain mill first, then the bank.

"Lilybell married Felix, thinking he was in partnership with the colonel, only to find when her husband died that it was the sole property of Wayne cutter, the colonel's nephew, lock, stock, and beer barrels.

"By this time Lilybell realized her hubby had been a total liar, a man who jollied up the crowds, played the big shot, and on top of that, had an incurably wandering eye."

I suspected it was something well below his eye that did the roving.

On the day Felix died, he had come home drunk after 2:00 A.M. Lilybell's letter to Iva had said he was so far gone he fell asleep on the couch while she was yelling at him. She stormed off to bed in the spare room, and when she got up a few hours later, found him dead on the floor beside the couch.

"She told me she had him cremated" said Iva, "because that's what he'd told her he wanted. The family denies it. They claim she seduced the doctor into saying heart failure caused the death, then had Felix cremated to hide the murder."

Iva shook her head sorrowfully, straightened up a little, and looked me in the eye. "I think you can see it's more likely she went to Corden to get away from all the headaches, not as any favor to me."

"Felix ever have any problems with his heart before he died?" I asked.

"It depends on who you talk to. Some say yes, others say no. Lilybell claimed he'd had spells, and the doctor confirms that—but of course the Fox men won't accept his word."

"Who'd she think Felix had been messing around with?"

"Well, there was at least one of his waitresses, maybe more. And Lilybell was convinced he'd been chasing a married cousin. I'm not sure about any of this—she told me such wild stories all the time I could never be sure how much to swallow."

"Got any names?"

"I think the waitress was Patsy something. The cousin was Imogene Coy."

"What's happened to Felix's beer and pool parlor?"

"Oh, it still operates under the old name, the Fox Lounge. A Fox cousin manages it, but Wayne still owns it."

I tried taking her back to questions about the death of her father. She scowled and shook her head.

"I'm sorry, but I've talked too many times about all that. I just can't go into it anymore. For heaven's sake, I was only six years old—I can't drag all of that up again. It was a totally terrifying time, the wind shook the house, and Mother was about out of her mind. She kept telling us to sleep, everything

would be fine in the morning, don't worry. Only she was so
frantic it scared us both about half to death. I don't want to
think about it anymore."

A LITTLE BEFORE noon, after lunch in a counter joint,
I headed back for Corden. It was too late to try for Sioux Falls,
and it occurred to me that Margaret would be at the hotel. We
hadn't seen each other since the high school reunion murders, about a year back. She was sitting in the lobby with Ma
when I came in, and she offered a smile with some promise.

To my surprise, Ma suddenly decided she had to check
with Bertha about something in the kitchen and left us alone.

"I thought you were supposed to be in Aberdeen," said
Margaret.

"Already been. Going to Sioux Falls tomorrow. How you
doing?"

"Just fine." She raised her left hand and flashed a rock
of immodest size on her ring finger.

I whistled, sat down, and started rolling a smoke.

"How come a guy forking over that much ice lets you out
of sight?"

"He knows it's only for a couple weeks, and he isn't the
jealous type. Has great self-confidence. Almost your equal."

"In everything?"

"Everything that counts."

I lit the cigarette and grinned. "Okay, you got me. How'd
Ma con you into coming back?"

"She said she needed me—and you'd be out of town a
couple weeks."

"Was the persuader—that I'd be gone?"

"We never fought," she reminded me. "You left to paint
signs, I went back home. I never had any illusions about you."

She was enough to make me wonder what kept me on the road.

"So what's this guy who's ringed you do that makes him rich enough for a rock like that?"

"He's a lawyer. And that's all you need to know. Tell me what you're working on now."

I did, and she asked if I'd been involved with Lilybell. I admitted I'd had ideas, but no chances, since she died the night we met.

"So, you're bound to avenge her, huh?"

"Something like that."

Engaged women I've known usually take a tolerant, superior attitude toward free men, and it doesn't exactly charm my ass off. But I couldn't resist asking Margaret to take a walk with me after dusk. To my surprise, she agreed.

"How come?" I asked when we reached the edge of town and stopped, facing each other.

"How come what?"

"You agreed to this walk?"

She laughed. "Because you asked, and I remember we had very nice times once. I know I could never take you seriously—you're a compulsive gypsy, a womanizing opportunist with no morals and lots of bad habits. But you can be very funny, and in your way you respect and like me. Maybe it's something bad in me that makes you so attractive. You're the only man who ever made love to me and acted as if it were important for me to enjoy it all too. That's more exceptional than you can believe."

"Margaret, you're giving me big ideas."

"I'm not surprised. Do you know the west wing apartment is empty again?"

"No."

"It is. We can go there if you like."

I told her like didn't half cover it. We walked back down

the hill with some speed, did a roundabout approach to the hotel from the rear, and slipped into the apartment. A few years before I'd taken a partner into rooms next door and found a young couple busy on the bed. If they'd been in the way this time, it would have been fatal for them.

Happily the bed was empty. Lots of women in my life have been more acrobatic and energetic than Margaret, but she was the warmest, most loving, most appreciative of any. I wasn't just satisfied, drained, and proud, it was better than having punched out the biggest bully in the bar and having the whole mob cheering. When it was over we just hung on to each other, not giving a damn if dawn never showed.

THE TRIP TO Sioux Falls was long enough to wear off
the glow from the night before. A cold wind whistled across
the prairie from the north, rolling tumbleweeds faster than
my Model T would go and whipping dust across the landscape
so thickly that normal dust tail raised by my jalopy was hardly
noticeable. All the cars and trucks I met had their windows
rolled up tight, and the drivers' lips were straight lines across
their faces, with maybe a sag at the corners. They squinted
as if afraid the dust would coat their eyeballs and blind them.

Some states have trees that turn bright colors and make
folks sentimental about fall. In South Dakota about the only
trees around are windbreaks near farmhouses, and they don't
go in for any of that nonsense. Cottonwoods turn yellow, elms
get a burned brown, and box elders hang on to dark, dry green
leaves until real freezing shrivels and drops them to blow
across the frozen earth.

It was early lunchtime when I hit town and stopped at a
gas station to fill up and ask directions to the Fox Lounge.
The directions were good; I found the place set back from the

highway, with over half a dozen jalopies and pickup trucks scattered in the parking lot out front.

There were about a dozen guys in the place, half of them at the bar, the others at tables close by. A flouncy waitress served the tables, and a beaver-faced man tended bar. I took a table near the kitchen door by the end of the bar and started rolling a smoke. The waitress jiggled my way.

I ordered a ham sandwich and draft beer and asked if she was Patsy.

She said coming right up, and no.

She spoke to the bartender as he filled my beer mug, and glanced my way. His small, beady eyes blinked solemnly. It didn't seem likely he owned a smile.

When she delivered my beer I asked her name.

"Edie," she said, and left.

A good share of the guys around were rubbernecking my way by the time I got my cigarette going and gave the beer a try.

When Edie brought the sandwich, I asked if Patsy worked here anymore.

"Nope. She's at Basil's, downtown."

"What's her last name?"

"Eldridge. You got any more questions?"

"No ma'am, thank you very kindly."

"Don't mention it."

Edie talked to four guys at a table near the entrance, and one of them facing me leaned forward and spoke to a giant sitting across from him. The giant slowly turned to glower at me. He had a cigar stub in his face. I grinned.

He got up. It took him longer than average because he was half again bigger than average. I glanced at the bartender. He was busy polishing a glass.

The monster came my way, halted by my table, and casually dropped his cigar butt in my beer mug. I leaned back in my chair to keep from kinking my neck as I took in his face. It was wide-cheeked, blocky-chinned, and had a nose that somewhere along the years had lost track of directions. His eyes had the cold blankness of a dalmatian.

"What're you lookin' for, rube?" he asked in a voice like a rusty saw.

"A friendly bar."

"You look like you need one. Who busted your nose?"

"I don't think it was the one that did yours. You want to gab, sit down—you're too damned big to gawk up at."

"You ain't going to be around long enough to get a kink in your neck. Haul ass."

"Don't tell me, you're the bouncer here, right?"

"If you don't move, you'll bounce."

I sighed, started up easy, then flipped the table so the far edge bounced off his shins and crashed down on his toes. He bellowed like a gored steer and threw the table aside, which made it easy for me to step in and spear him just above the nuts. That brought his chin in range, and I worked on it.

Things might've gone bad then, because his jaw was delicate as a sledgehammer head, but the table to the toes had done real damage and he was having a hell of a time staying on his feet. Another shot to the privates brought him down low enough so I was able to bring my head up under his jaw and stretch him.

I paid Edie for the service and sustenance, handed a five to the bartender for the mess, and walked out.

Nobody coaxed me to stay.

7

BASIL'S CAFÉ WAS busy when I arrived, but I was
lucky enough to catch a booth left by an early diner. Within
seconds a waitress approached briskly with a smile bright
enough to light a cave. I asked what was special.

"Our hot pork sandwich with potatoes and gravy is good
as any you've ever tasted."

"Your name Patsy?"

"That's right, how'd you know?"

"Edie at the Fox Lounge told me."

The smile lost some wattage.

"Really? How'd she happen to tell you about me?" She
was trying to sound casual, but without any luck.

"I asked. And since you recommend the hot pork sandwich, I'll take it. With coffee."

"You won't be sorry," she said, and moved off.

Soon she was back with my order, which smelled as good
as promised. The smile had recovered some. After she'd put
down the sandwich and coffee, she crossed her hands above

her waist and asked how come I'd happened to be asking about her at the Lounge.

"It's kind of involved. Can I talk with you a little after the noon rush is off?"

She glanced around at the crowd, looked back at me, and finally said all right.

By the time I was having a second cup of coffee and a smoke the crowd had thinned, and Patsy, after a brief conference with a man behind the counter, came over and stood by my booth.

"Why'd you want to talk with me?"

"It starts with a woman named Lilybell Fox."

"Oh," she said, and suddenly slipped onto the bench across from me and folded her hands tightly on the table.

"You heard what happened to her?" I asked.

She nodded. "Everybody's talking about it. It's awful. Are you a cop?"

"Something like. Checking a few angles. The story we hear is that Felix had a couple girlfriends. Some say you were one of them. Is that right?"

She took a deep breath, frowned, and drew back. "That is not right. Felix was interested in me and any other woman around. That doesn't mean all of them were interested back. I'm not the kind that takes passes from married men, and that's why I left the lounge well before he died."

"You been in town regular past week?"

"That's right. And I can prove it."

"Fine. You know any women around the lounge who weren't fussy about a little hanky-panky with a married man?"

"Edie wasn't."

"Anybody else?"

"Nobody I knew. He flirted with any woman, but if he was really fooling with anybody away from the lounge, it wouldn't be anything I'd know about. The thing with Edie was so obvious you could be blind and not miss it. She wanted him to leave Lilybell and marry her. She wouldn't ever just fool around."

"Didn't you ever hear about him and a cousin?"

She frowned deeper.

"I suppose you mean Imogene Coy. Yes, there was some talk about her. I never paid any attention, and I don't believe it's true. Imogene's too blamed proud to get messed up with a man like Felix. And she sure never hung out at the lounge."

"She married?"

"Uh-huh. To Percy Coy. He was crippled about ten years ago—tractor tipped on him—lives in a wheelchair. Imogene works in the county courthouse as a secretary. Actually, she's more like an assistant to the county commissioner. She's real smart, and a hard worker. No time for fooling around."

"What made Lilybell figure you were messing with Felix?"

"I don't know. He probably made claims. That'd be just like him. I think he got more kick out of bragging about making out than actually doing it."

"Where'd Felix ever get a shot at Imogene?"

"Well, that's just it—he wouldn't. They didn't even see each other in church. He was a Catholic, and she's a Lutheran. He probably saw her on the street now and again and heard all about her work for the county and wanted to seem important himself."

"What do you know about the husband in the wheelchair?"

"Percy? Not much. He gets around more than you might expect a man in a wheelchair could. He was a very big, strong man once and still has the broad shoulders, and his face is nice. Sort of wide and friendly. He did pretty good as a farmer, before he was crippled. I've heard he's smart as his wife, goes to the library a lot."

Patsy got the Coy's home address and telephone number

for me before I left the café. I found a phone booth in a hotel and called the number. The answering voice was low, almost hoarse.

I told him my name and asked if he'd let me come around to talk with him.

"What about?"

"Your wife, Felix Fox, his wife, Lilybell, and murder."

There was a quiet pause, then he laughed. "Well, you kind of get to the point, don't you? Okay, come around. You got the address? Fine. Just walk in. You go through the first door on the left off the hall. I'll be waiting."

It was a medium house for Sioux Falls. White clapboard, two dormers on the second floor, a wide, unscreened porch with two wicker chairs up against the wall. I went up the two steps to the porch, passed through the storm and inner door, and called hello.

Percy Coy sat in his wheelchair in the far corner beside an end table stacked with books. He was smoking a goosenecked pipe and stared over small reading glasses at me. His face was wide, muscular, and clean-shaven. Wrinkles framed his wide mouth and made crinkles around the dark blue eyes that examined me with a shrewd squint. He waved me toward the brown couch to his left.

I parked, brought out my fixings, and started rolling a cigarette. He watched and waited.

"You know what happened to Lilybell Fox?" I asked.

"I know she was murdered."

"I first met and talked with her the night before that happened. She was trying to find out why Iva Cutter's ma got cut off from her kids after her husband died in a snowstorm a long while back. You know that story?"

"Sounds familiar, but fill me in fresh."

I did.

He smoked and watched me.

"Did you ever hear," I asked, "that the ma, Mattie Cutter, sort of helped her husband die in the snow during that blizzard?"

"I heard he wasn't your model husband."

"How about Felix's death? You ever hear he maybe got some help dying?"

"With a man like Felix, I'd guess you could figure murder would be death by a natural cause."

"You ever hear stories about him messing with your wife?"

"Nobody's told me a story like that. I'm a cripple, you know?"

"Okay. You think it could've happened?"

He seemed to consider the question seriously. Finally he shook his head.

"Not likely. It'd be too hard to handle even if she was interested. And if Imogene got interested in some other man, it sure wouldn't be a tinhead like Felix. She's a compulsive worker, always down to business. Wasting time gives her the horrors. You might think she'd get restless, being married to me. Fact is, I've worried about that some, but she's never given me any cause to get suspicious. We're close. We talk things out."

"You know Patsy, the waitress who used to be at the lounge, now works at Basil's?"

He nodded.

"It's interesting. She told me she couldn't believe your wife ever messed with Felix. Saw her about the same way you do. You ever hear that this Patsy was into it with Felix?"

"I think that's a story one of the other waitresses passed around."

"Edie?"

He glanced at me sharply. "Yeah. You talked with her too?"

"I try to talk with everybody. What time's your wife get off work?"

"Five or close."

"What's she wearing?"

"Blue dress, black shoes. No hat. You figure to be waiting when she leaves the county courthouse?"

"Uh-huh."

"Don't make a pass. I'd hate to have to run over you in my wheelchair."

8

IMOGENE'S BLUE-AND-WHITE dress fit her slim body without sags or bulging. It made me think of her burly husband and wonder how women manage under men that size. Seems like they'd feel squashed.

She walked fast, with a no-nonsense stride, and I had to move smart to keep up.

"Mrs. Coy?"

She glanced at me and kept walking.

"I've been talking with Percy," I said. "He told me where and when you got off work and what you'd be wearing so I could talk with you."

That got me a glance that suggested Percy would have some explaining to do.

"I'm working on the Lilybell Fox murder."

She came to a halt and faced me. Her gray eyes were large under long, pale lashes, and they took me in with a sharp disapproval.

"What's that got to do with me?"

"There'd been some talk that you and her husband were cozy before he died."

"And you've decided that since there's also talk he didn't die of natural causes, maybe I killed his wife?"

"Nope. Just want to get the whole story. Your husband doesn't think you were involved, and neither does Patsy, but you're the only one who can really know, so I'm asking you."

She started walking again, and I went along. After a few steps she began talking without looking at me.

"I was never involved with the man. He did exactly what you have just done, waited for me when I left work and walked along, talking. He claimed he'd heard that certain county authorities were getting complaints against his bar, and he wanted to know if I'd heard anything because he wanted to head off any problems. He claimed he ran a clean place, never served juveniles, and allowed no fooling around with his help. I told him in no uncertain terms that I'd never heard anything about his crummy bar, and if I had, I wouldn't be telling him anything about it."

"What'd he say to that?"

"He got very upset and said there was nothing crummy about his bar, some of the best people in town used it, and I had no idea what I was talking about because I'd never been there.

"Of course he was right, and I admitted it. But I still insisted I wasn't about to tell him everything heard in the courthouse. That calmed him some, and he became apologetic, saying he didn't mean to sound as if he expected me to betray confidences, but he was very anxious to learn if things had gone on in the lounge behind his back. He gave me a great line about my wonderful reputation in the courthouse, said he'd heard how important I was to the commissioner and how much influence I had in county government, and insisted he had to try every possible way to get to the bottom of things."

We stopped at a crossing and waited as a Model A drove

by. She stared across the street while I watched her profile. It could have used a little more nose and less chin, but was pretty fine all the same, and she knew it.

"Are you really that much on the inside of things?" I asked.

She lowered her chin and turned her head.

"I generally know what's going on. For example, I know you were in a brawl with Tiny Fox at the lounge today."

"Know why?"

"Ostensibly it was because he tried to throw you out."

"What makes a brawl at the lounge news in the courthouse?"

"Involvement with one of the Fox family is all it takes. Have you any idea what you're getting into?"

"I'm beginning to get a notion."

"The smartest thing you could do is get in your car and leave town. Now. I don't care what kind of terror you might be in a barroom brawl, you can't take on the whole Fox crowd in their own town."

"They really own the place?"

"No, far from it. But smart people don't cross them."

"Smart's never been my strong suit."

She smiled, showing small dimples and flashy teeth. "No, you're more into quick action and persistence, aren't you? How in the world did a man your size whip Tiny?"

"He's slow, and I'm sudden. So what came of your little talk with Felix?"

"Well, he walked me all the way home, and we parted at my front step."

"And you told him nothing about what you'd heard?"

"There was nothing to tell. No one I know or was around ever said anything about the lounge that even hinted Felix might be in trouble. After all, Wayne Cutter was the owner."

"So Felix was trying to feed you a line."

"Exactly."

"What was his next approach?"

"Look, I've got to get home and start dinner for Percy. If you must, come along and we'll talk while I work. Percy won't mind."

"And there's nothing he doesn't know about you and Felix?"

"Not a thing."

Percy was in his corner of the living room, reading, when we entered. He peered over his reading glasses at me, then at his wife.

"He had more questions than I could answer walking home, so I brought him in. Come along," she said to me. "I'll start dinner."

I followed her through the dining room into a kitchen bigger than average and neat as any I'd ever seen. She waved me toward a chair at a table against the back wall. A window overlooked a shallow yard and a row of elms out back.

Percy wheeled in while she was rummaging through a new refrigerator, pushed his chair into an empty space opposite me at the table, and grinned my way.

"How'd you manage it?" he asked.

"What?"

"To get invited in like this. I figured she'd cut you dead."

"He asked questions that made sense," she said as she hauled containers from the refrigerator and set them on the counter.

Percy looked at her and back at me. "How'd you like her answers so far?"

"Haven't got them all yet."

"You never will."

"Percy," said his wife, "please go back in the living room, okay? You'll just complicate things, and I want this finished before we eat."

His mouth smiled, but his eyes showed hurt. He carefully turned the wheelchair around and left us.

"We're going to have warmed-over hot dish," she told me. "There's not enough for three, so I can't ask you to eat with us."

"How long's he been crippled?"

"Ten years. Going on forever."

"Did you like it on the farm?"

"No. It's a life for a drudge or a saint. He loved it. Worked himself to death from spring through fall and spent the winter reading. I think he reads less now than he did then. That's the perversity of human nature."

"How'd Felix work on you after the first meeting?"

"By telephone. He called me at work and here."

"About what?"

"My irresistible appeal. His obsession with me."

"You talked with him?"

"Mostly I listened. It was stupid, but I did. He had a lot of imagination and could be very funny. He'd tell me stories he heard in the lounge and gossip he picked up about city hall and the county courthouse people I knew. At first I thought he was making it all up, but pretty soon I realized he was astonishingly observant and shrewd about people. He understood them all too well."

"Including you?"

She had the hot dish in the oven by then, and the table set for two.

"I'm not certain. I'd like to think I was too much for him. Certainly he wasn't a man I'd ever fall in love with. On the other hand, he was clever enough to intrude on me more than I ever should have allowed, and actually made me see through a few people in politics better than I ever had on my own."

"When did you start meeting with him?"

"What makes you think I did?"

"I don't think the stories about you and him would've been common if nothing more had happened than what you've told me."

She leaned her bottom against the counter, folded her arms, and managed to look almost apologetic.

"Okay, you're right. I met him just once in the park one bright winter night. It seemed safe because there was snow on the ground and no danger of getting seriously physical. I agreed to meet him because he threatened to visit the house if I refused, and I just didn't want that kind of a fuss. He told me all about how much he loved and needed me. It's amazing how many men think that's a compelling argument for getting a woman to bed."

"Percy know about all this?"

"He knew about the calls, of course. This house isn't big enough to keep that sort of thing secret when it becomes regular. I told him later about the meeting in the park because when Felix walked me home we saw a friend of Percy's, and I was sure the word would get back."

"How'd he take it?"

"He thought it was terribly funny. Percy thinks everything is funny. Even his condition. Maybe that's how he stays sane. If he is sane. There's nothing more I can tell you. I never was Felix Fox's mistress, I'm a little sorry he died, and I don't particularly suspect it was anything but natural. Now if you'll leave, we'll have supper."

9

THERE WAS NO Murdoff in the city directory, but there was a Colin Murduff. Given the man's lousy writing, it seemed reasonable his *u* had to look like an *o*.

My call was answered by a woman who sounded impatient. She said yes? in a no tone.

"Is Colin Murduff in?" I asked.

"No. He's working at the station. Want that number?"

"The address'd be fine."

She gave it to me grudgingly, and I drove around, figuring since it was located on the edge of town, the station was for gas and not police or firemen.

It was a Standard station. I pulled in beside the pumps and got out as a young man popped through the front door and trotted my way.

"Colin?" I asked.

"No sir. Want a fill and the oil checked?"

"Yeah. Where's Colin?"

"Oil pit. Inside."

I walked past the young man, entered the station, and

passed through the front area and into the back. A shining Chevy straddled the pit, and I hunkered down to peer at the legs of a man draining the oil pan.

"Colin Murduff?" I asked.

"You got me," he said in the voice of an obliging man. It couldn't have been more different than the voice of the Murdoff I'd heard at the hotel.

"Like to talk with you a minute."

"Shoot."

"You the only Murduff in town?"

He moved my way and peered up.

"Well now, except for the wife and a son I think is mine, yeah. Why?"

"No father or uncles?"

"Not in town. Got an uncle in Minneapolis."

"What's he look like?"

"Scrooge," he said, and laughed. "Why?"

"A man using your last name stayed in the Wilcox Hotel in Corden a couple nights ago. Left without paying for his room."

He blinked once, then grinned.

"That sounds like a stunt old Uncle Milt might've pulled twenty years ago, but he doesn't travel any these days. Been in a nursing home, flat on his back, for the last two years."

He moved to the ladder at the end of the pit, climbed out, and stood wiping his hands on an oily rag and grinning at me. His face was broad and soft, with the kind of black stubble beard that shows even after a fresh shave and buck teeth that wouldn't hide. He looked about forty-five.

"What're you?" he asked, "A bill collector?"

"In a way. I'm poking into the murder of a woman named Lilybell Fox."

He shook his head. "Uncle Milt didn't do it, I'll guarantee you."

"And he's the only living relative you've got?"

"Total supply. I'm like an old orphan."

"Got a customer drives a black Packard with a Sioux Falls license?"

His grin faded a little as he frowned in thought, and then he nodded. "Sure. Got two."

"Can you describe them?"

He offered descriptions with loving detail that made it clear neither of them was the man I'd seen.

"The dude who signed in as Murdoff," I said, "came the night Lilybell got killed and snuck out without being seen. He was taller than me, and I'd guess forty or so. Had bushy dark hair with touches of gray, bristly eyebrows, droopy lids, a mouth like a bear trap, and a voice like a rusty saw. Sound like any of your regulars?"

Concentrating must have hurt Colin. He got a pained expression for several seconds, and then it eased off and he was grinning again.

"Sure. Not a regular, but a fella like that was in a week ago. I remember because he asked who was in charge here, and when I said I was, he wanted my name. If I'd known he was gonna borrow it, I'd have lied."

"What was he driving?"

"Not sure—think it was a Chevy. Coupe."

"You ask why he wanted your name?"

"Naw."

"You ask for his?"

"He offered it. Jones. B. D. Jones. I asked was he related to Buck Jones, the cowboy actor, but he didn't think that was funny."

"That the only time he ever came around?"

"The only time when I was pumping."

At my request he brought out a notepad. I wrote down the address of the Corden County police station, gave him Joey's name, and asked him to telephone collect if the guy showed up again.

"Sure thing. I'll catch the license number and all. But I don't suppose he'll show again."

There was no B. D. Jones listed in the telephone directory, or any Jones with a first name beginning with a B. I wasn't surprised.

10

PATSY SPOTTED ME the moment I entered Basil's Café and hurried over with a worried frown as I slipped into a booth.

"What happened to the big smile?" I asked.

She glanced toward a table near the front and leaned close. "You're in big trouble," she whispered. "There are Fox cousins at the table over there. They'll be waiting when you leave."

"How many?"

"Four."

"Have they finished supper?"

She looked puzzled, glanced their way, and said they were having dessert.

"Good. Bring me the roast beef and coffee, okay?"

"If you're smart," she said earnestly, "you'll go back as though heading for the men's and just keep going through the kitchen and out the back door."

"I'm too hungry. Maybe after I eat, okay?"

She raised her eyes to the ceiling, shrugged, took my order, and headed for the kitchen.

I took my time eating, and the food was okay but the coffee seemed bitter. The dessert, apple pie with just the right amount of cinnamon and a scoop of ice cream on the side, would have been perfect if it hadn't had apple seed husks in it, but I picked them out and didn't complain. When Patsy came to refill my coffee cup, I asked if the Fox men were still waiting.

"Yes. But it's too late to try the back. Two of them left, and I'm sure they've gone around back to catch you if you go that way."

"How about you call the cops?"

"That wouldn't help anything. There's one across the street, watching. He's Tiny Fox's kid brother."

"Is there a Fox cop out back?"

"I think this is the only one on the force."

I thanked her, put down a two-bit tip, and slipped out of the booth. The front table was deserted now, but two guys stood on the sidewalk by the front window, smoking and casually watching the door.

I headed for the back at a quick pace, shoved through the kitchen's swinging door, spotted a cleaver on a butcher's block, snatched it in passing, and headed for the door. A short character in a stained apron stared at me with his mouth open.

The back yard was half shaded by a box elder. Two guys who'd been leaning against its trunk moved to cut me off, grinning broadly. They were nowhere near as big as Tiny.

I headed for them, lifting the cleaver just above my waist. Both raised open hands and backed off. I charged. They took off in opposite directions.

I darted back to the kitchen door and flattened against the wall beside it. When the third Fox popped out, I clipped the back of his noggin with the flat of the blade, then buried my right fist in his follower's belly.

Back in the kitchen, I put the cleaver on the block, thanked the cook, and left by the front door. The cop across the street stared some and started toward the café as I went to my car.

Nobody followed me.

11

MARGARET WAS READING in the lobby of the Wilcox Hotel when I got back to Corden. She greeted me with a warm smile.

"Waiting up?" I asked.

"Of course. Did you learn anything?"

"Not sure. Anybody been in room ten?"

"Bertha made up the bed fresh, that's all. It hasn't been used."

"Luggage still there?"

She nodded.

"I'm going up to take a look at it."

"May I come along?"

"Why not?"

We entered the room, which smelled faintly of talcum powder. One suitcase was open on the rack. The other was on the floor by the bed.

"How about you look through the open one," I said to Margaret, "and I'll check this other one."

"I think Joey's been through them."

"Yeah, but he's squeamish about handling women's stuff, so I think it's worth taking another shot at it."

"They must weigh a ton," said Margaret as she began lifting books out. "There's a whole library here."

She spread the books. They seemed to be all detective stories—Conan Doyle, Agatha Christie, Ellery Queen, and some others.

My case also had books lining the bottom. Mark Twain, Henry James, Scott Fitzgerald, and six volumes of The New Practical Reference Library in brown leather bindings.

"Well," I said, "when she told me she came to Corden for tranquillity, it sounded like she was just being cute, but maybe she really did mean to settle here."

While I was shuffling through the books, looking for possible insertions or notes, Margaret was poking around in the clothing she'd stacked beside the suitcase.

"Here's something," she said, holding up a dark blue robe as she reached into the pocket. Her hand emerged with a fat booklet. "It's a diary."

"Let's see."

She held it back, frowning. "It doesn't seem fair. Diaries are so terribly personal."

"Come on, Margaret, you think she'd rather save her privacy than have her murderer caught?"

"I almost think I would, if it were me."

"Okay, what'll we do, burn it? That'd probably be illegal, and Joey'd be madder than hell if he ever found out. And for all you know, Lilybell might've been keeping a written record just so if anything happened to her, we'd know what it was all about."

"All right, let's take it downstairs. I don't like being here where she was killed."

I closed the door behind us, locked it, followed her to the

lobby, and suggested she do the reading, starting with the last pages.

She sat in a rocker across from me, opened the book at the end, and leafed back slowly a few pages before she began reading. Almost at once she smiled and glanced up.

"You want to hear the last paragraph? It's about you."

I was going to have to read it all, but figured there was plenty of time. I nodded to humor her.

She began reading in a soft, low voice. " 'He's not tall or handsome, but has wonderful dark eyes, a quick wit, and, as Fitzgerald described Tom Buchanan in *The Great Gatsby*, "a body capable of enormous leverage—a cruel body." He pretends to be a bumpkin while he watches and listens, missing nothing. I think this is going to be fun.' "

"When'd the diary start?" I asked.

She turned to the first page.

"June sixteenth, this year."

"What's she say?"

She skimmed the first page and turned to the next.

"She says Felix has been dead a month, and she still isn't able to write about it. That eventually she will but she will have to wait awhile yet, to figure out her feelings and try to understand him and herself. Then she writes about how the Fox family shuns her, and there's no one she can talk to. She needs a goal, something to occupy her mind, and decides to learn what she can about the family she married into."

I watched as her eyes scanned the page and then another.

"Now we're getting into it," said Margaret. "She's writing about Colonel Cutter. Wonders how he managed to come to South Dakota after the Civil War, stake a claim, go through two consecutive years of failed crops because of drouth and grasshoppers, and suddenly show up in Corden with money enough to start a business."

"Just read it to me."

Lilybell had obviously been a critically suspicious woman. She commented acidly on the short history of Corden written by the colonel and published in 1910. According to the old man, Lilybell wrote, every Corden pioneer had been the soul of honesty, integrity, and industriousness. She suspected they were in fact all pirates and opportunists, and the colonel a model for the lot of them.

She wrote that Victor, the colonel's older brother, had joined forces with Cole Fox to complete the trio of unscrupulous abusers and exploiters of women.

"They multiplied like maggots," she wrote, "and infested the whole area."

"A little personal prejudice there," I commented. "The colonel, from all I know, had only one kid, and his brother only had the two. It was the Fox family that multiplied."

Lilybell wrote bitterly about her husband, Felix, being a patsy for everyone. His father and Wayne Cutter kept Felix on as chief bartender and caretaker on a salary, taking advantage of his natural talent for attracting people and being the perfect host to the public, while letting everyone believe the place was a generous gift to him. Lilybell's resentment of the exploitation and phoniness just about curled the pages of the diary, but she included a great deal of self—ridicule for having failed to recognize Felix as a hollow man from the beginning.

"My only excuse," she wrote, "was that I was so awfully young when we met, and he was so damned good-looking and seemed wildly infatuated with me; naturally I assumed he must be bright, good, and noble as well as handsome."

Later on she wrote, "It is easy to understand why Mattie let Victor freeze in the blizzard. He was a brute to her and the children, but worse, he was a fool. While he struggled on the claim, his brother lived comfortably in town and established himself as a businessman and community leader. He could easily have brought Victor and his family in and given them a decent life."

At another point she observed: "Men are only stronger than women because of size and muscle. Women's strength comes from greater character, intelligence, and patience."

"What happened to her husband?" Margaret asked as she lowered the diary to her lap.

"Supposedly died of a heart attack after a drunk night."

"At home?"

"Alone with Lilybell."

"You think she arranged it?"

"Could be. The body was cremated as soon as she could manage it."

"Is the colonel still alive?"

"Nope. Been gone about a dozen years or more."

"So who's the family dictator now?"

"His nephew, the Wayne Lilybell refers to. I've got to learn more about him."

12

I TRIED TO convince Margaret that a conference in my room would do us both good, but it didn't sell. She left for sweet solitary rest in the room over the kitchen next to Bertha's.

That left me with the diary. Near the end, before Lilybell's comments about me, she wrote of plans to look up Wilda Mahon, who lived in Fulton, a town just north of the road between Aquatown and Corden.

The drive to Fulton next morning took about twenty minutes. Wind out of the northwest battered the car, making me fight the wheel to stay on the road. The sky was naked clear, the prairie desolate and endless in every direction. I made the north turn just east of a low hill and headed into a shallow valley, where the village squatted beside a sad lake, shrunk to little more than a murky puddle. The gas station in midtown had two pumps standing in front of a deserted-looking shack. As I pulled in, an old-timer shuffled out to meet me, grinning like a chimp.

"Know a lady named Wilda Mahon?" I asked as he started filling my tank.

"Yup." He tipped his head north. "Lives in the white house over there. You kin?"

I shook my head while wondering how often he got to fill a gas tank out here.

Minutes later I parked in front of the small white house. Paint was peeling from the porch's square pillars and had disappeared from its shrinking board floor.

My knock on the door echoed, and it didn't seem likely there was life inside, but after a few seconds the inner door opened and a woman with streaked gray hair appeared behind the storm door window.

Our heads were on the same level, and her sharp blue eyes examined my mug and clothes with something like tolerant amusement. Her skin was surprisingly smooth, her mouth wide, with laugh wrinkles at the corners, and her teeth, only slightly shown by her smile, were white and even. Her hair was smoothly brushed, and she had a small but firm chin.

"Well," she said, "I don't guess you're here selling vacuum cleaners or brushes."

"No ma'am. If you're Wilda Mahon, I'd like to talk with you about Lilybell Fox."

She glanced over my shoulder at the Model T, then gave me a shrewd squint.

"You're not with the police."

"I am in a way. Helping out Joey Paxton, the Corden cop. You know what happened to Lilybell in our town?"

"Tell me."

"She was murdered in the Wilcox Hotel Sunday night— or maybe early Monday. Stabbed to death on her bed. We found a diary in her luggage that says she was going to come and visit you, trying to learn things about the Cutter family."

"Ah." She shoved the storm door open, and waved me into her small living room. A potbellied stove faced the door, showing a flickering redness through isinglass. On its right a black coal scuttle was half filled with briquets. The room was warm and smelled of coffee.

"Sit," she said, jerking her head toward an ancient dark brown couch with wooden arms.

"Hadn't you heard about the murder?" The stiff leather of the couch creaked under me.

She nodded. "I just wanted to hear what you'd say."

"How'd she know you?"

"We were third cousins. She was a bright little thing, full of the devil and wild ideas. Stayed one summer with me when her Daddy went west looking for work after they lost their farm. Her mother stayed with the Elrods, in Corden. You want coffee?"

She brought it in a white mug on a tray with sugar and cream on the side. It had been kept hot too long. She drank it straight and scalding from a shallow white porcelain cup. I loaded it up with cream and sugar.

"Did you like her?" I asked, settling back.

"Of course. She gave me the liveliest summer of my life. I can't say I ever got to know her well when she was a grown woman, but we met now and again. She was getting plump, wasn't she?"

"Some."

"You men like women that way, don't you? I remember my husband saying on our honeymoon night that my legs were like toothpicks. I told him if he didn't like them he could look the other way."

"Did he?"

She sniffed. "All husbands look the other way—usually toward somebody like Lilybell."

"Was she a flirt?"

"You say you met her, and you don't know? What do you want from me?"

"Anything you can tell me about Colonel Cutter and Cole Fox."

"Well, that'd cover a lot of ground. If you were to ask just about anybody from the old days, they'd tell you the colonel was Christ and Cole was his Paul, and they made Corden the Holy Land. That might be hard to swallow when you look at it today, but that's what folks liked to think fifteen, twenty years ago and more."

"In her diary, Lilybell wondered how come those two guys came out of the Civil War, showed up here, started farming on claims, lost everything to drouth and grasshoppers, and suddenly turned into successful businessmen in town. How'd they swing it?"

"Well, believe me, it wasn't as easy as you make it sound. The one sure thing is, the colonel had style and brass, and Cole had the gift of gab and the soul of a pimp. He could coax money out of a beggar and convince him he'd done him a favor."

"You knew them well, then?"

"Oh yes. We, my husband and I, were the sort of little people the colonel and Cole were kind to. My husband, Delbert, was a carpenter, a blamed good one, and he did very well. Everybody wanted houses and barns built, and he kept a crew busy right up to when he fell off a barn roof. It didn't kill him quick, but he got creeping paralysis that killed him before the year was out."

"A while back, huh?"

"Over thirty years."

For a second she lost her lightness. She sipped coffee and asked if I wanted more. I shook my head.

"So you don't know where the colonel's money came from?"

"Providence, more than likely. The colonel was born to be rich. One of those men with God on his side."

"Ever hear any stories about Felix's death being fishy?"

"Of course. It wasn't really all straight out, but a good many observed how handy it was for Lilybell, who never had

got on with him after their first year, what with his carrying
on and being basically a bum."

"How about the story of Mattie and her husband, Victor?
You think she killed him?"

"Cold killed him. The blizzard. It wouldn't surprise me a
great deal if she turned a mite forgetful, or got distracted by
one of the kiddies and didn't get around to signal him back
to the house, but I'd never believe she did it on purpose.
Mattie didn't have the gumption for that. Never would've
stayed with that brute if she'd had an ounce of good sense or
backbone."

"I guess Victor wasn't as smart as the colonel."

"Victor didn't have sense enough to pour piss out of a
boot if the directions were on the heel."

She said that with enough heat to make me wonder what
her personal relationship might have been, but I decided not
to push it.

"You know any kin of the Cutters or Foxes that's some
taller than me and older, with scraggly eyebrows, mean eyes,
near floppy ears, and a big jaw?"

"Sounds like Uriah Hack."

"Who's he?"

"A shirttail relation of the Cutters. He was a wild kid,
always in trouble at school—finally got expelled. Went to the
Cities, and there was talk about him working as a strike
breaker during the big labor troubles in Minneapolis. Seems
like he killed a man, maybe more than one, in the riots there."

"He been in this territory lately?"

"Not that I know of. Why?"

"A guy like I described came to the hotel the same night
Lilybell signed in. A waitress at the café told me he looked
daggers at Lilybell when he saw her having supper there, and
after I found Lilybell's body in the morning, we found he'd
skipped in the night."

"How was she murdered?"

"Stabbed with something like an ice pick."

"Well, isn't that interesting? I seem to remember hearing that Uriah had two favorite tools when he was working as a strike breaker in Minneapolis. One was a blackjack, which he used for persuasion. For the real clincher, I understand, he relied on an ice pick."

13

WILDA HAD BEEN living in Fulton since the twenties, she said, when Wayne Cutter offered her the house which Wilda's husband had built. It was one of many places owned by the colonel in Corden County and was originally rented to a boozing doctor who drifted in when Fulton showed faint promise of being a busy village. After three years the doctor died of alcoholic poisoning, according to local gossip, and the house had a variety of renters until it became vacant and Wilda moved in.

"Why'd Wayne Cutter offer you the place?"

She laughed. "You can be blamed sure it wasn't for sweet charity. Mainly it was because I'd been taken into the colonel's family after Delbert died. The colonel's wife, Suellen, didn't like cooking and hated housekeeping, so he had no trouble convincing her it'd be Christian to let me take over both jobs, which would keep me too busy for mourning and free her to gad about as she pleased. Which pleased her silly. In fact, it worked so well the colonel bragged about it more than was smart, and that started gossip about us that embarrassed Wayne real bad. He figured moving me to Fulton would make him look big and might hush up all the talk."

"Was there anything to the gossip?" I asked.

She smiled sweetly.

"A bit. You have to understand that after Delbert died, I wasn't myself for quite a while. There was no insurance, we only rented our house, and I was left with this bitty pension that came from his service in the Spanish-American War. It was enough to survive on, only if I was careful, but there were expenses of the funeral and the doctoring before Delbert died, and the colonel paid for all of that. I was so grateful it just didn't seem possible to put him off when he got lovey. Especially when his wife was off at church doings and women's clubs about half the time and didn't care a stitch about the colonel's interests."

I guessed adultery must have hurt her more than she cared to admit, and she'd been ashamed to find she got a kick out of an affair with a rich older man. When the glow wore off, she'd felt guilt and disgust.

"So Wayne made you the offer to avoid more gossip when the colonel turned things over to him, and you accepted to clear your conscience?"

She frowned and straightened up.

"Nonsense. I didn't take to the notion of nursing a lecherous old man into his senility, which I could see was going to be the case all too blamed soon. Accepting the house was a perfect out for me"

So much for guilt.

"Did Wayne ever make a pass at you?"

"Don't be silly. Old men mess with younger women, never the other way around—unless the woman's rich as a skunk."

I grinned in agreement and asked if it was okay to smoke.

"I don't care if you burn." She got up, giving me a return grin.

"When did you first come to South Dakota?" I asked as she returned from the kitchen with her coffee cup refilled.

"In my ninth year. All the way from New York State. Crossed the plains in a covered wagon. I remember walking beside it and playing with other boys and girls in the caravan. The weather was mostly good that summer, or if it wasn't, I must have blanked out the bad days, because there are none in my memory. We weren't attacked by Indians or wolves, and I don't remember seeing any buffalo. Some deer, and lots of birds, prairie dogs, a few snakes, and millions of grasshoppers, and at night, moths. There were no dust storms that summer. The people on the trail were like family, close and excited about the future. It was just all dreamy to us kids. I guess ours was about the last of the wagon trains. I felt I was very lucky."

"Did the colonel ever talk about what he did in the Civil War?"

"No. It's funny, when I think about it, but when he and Cole Fox got together, they jawed about business, politics, and family doings. Maybe they talked war when they were drinking late together, or joined other veterans."

"Did they see action?"

"Oh yes, I did hear that much. They would have liked to make us think they won the war, but come right down to it, they never laid out any gory tales of the battles or killing they saw. Mostly I think they were happier just forgetting about it. I remember hearing the colonel was in the siege of Atlanta, near the war's end."

"When did he die?"

"Five years ago. He was eighty-two."

"How about Cole Fox?"

"Before him, about three years, I think, maybe more."

"Was he younger than the colonel?"

"Some. I'm not sure how much."

"I take it he wasn't rich when they met?"

"No. From all I can gather, his income came directly from the colonel in salaries and bonuses. He had no personal stock in the businesses, so there was nothing left to his heirs. You can imagine how well that went over with the Fox clan. They didn't feel a bit sweeter about it all going to Wayne Cutter when the colonel died. The grain elevator, the bank, real estate, and things like the Fox Lounge, they were all Wayne's."

"Lilybell was one of the big resenters, wasn't she? Because she thought her husband, Felix, should have got the lounge."

"Oh yes, she was bitter, no mistake. What galled her most was Felix being dumb enough to let the colonel take advantage. Although frankly, I suspect he never pretended the place would go to Felix. Felix just pretended to believe it would be his."

"I hear Felix was a great ladies' man—you think Lilybell ever tried getting even?"

"If the chance came along, probably. She wasn't a doormat type. Had lots of spirit."

"Enough to kill Felix?"

"Only the Fox crowd is dumb enough to believe that. If he'd been stabbed, shot, or hit with a frying pan, I could believe she was the one, but she simply wasn't the type to plot it out in cold blood and pretend it was heart failure. The family hated her because she was independent and never kowtowed to any of them. When they snooted her, she wasn't hurt, she was scornful. Wouldn't take a backseat to anybody."

"What do you think of the notion she was set on proving that the colonel was a crook? That she was going to expose him and the whole clan, and they felt vulnerable and brought in the ice pick artist to shut her up? Could Wayne Cutter have been shook up enough for that?"

"Absolutely. He's a man who always wanted power, and

he's thin-skinned as a new frog. Can't stand a word against anybody in the family, especially the colonel. I wouldn't put anything past Wayne."

"Know anybody in the family that Uriah might be close to?"

"Not now. I'd guess Felix was the only one who ever made allowances for him and kept in touch. You won't have much luck talking with him."

And it would be just as tough talking with the person who'd known Felix best, Lilybell. Nothing but dead ends.

"Know anybody connected with the Cutter crowd that's not happy with Wayne being king of the clan?"

She frowned thoughtfully. "Like somebody carrying a grudge?"

"That'd help."

"You might try Toby Tobiason. He's married to a daughter of the colonel's, who came with some other shirttail Cutter relatives."

"That's the photographer?"

She nodded.

"What's his gripe?"

"He's a proud man who's always been treated like a leech by the rest of the family. He manages to be polite to them, but you watch close and you can see the hate. It burns inside him."

14

MY OLD MAN, Elihu, came to the dining room table in his wheelchair each day at 6:00 P.M. and grumped through his supper. He was the kind who could make you feel guilty about having two good legs when his didn't work. Margaret was all concern and thoughtfulness; Ma watched him critically. We were having corn on the cob that night, which is Elihu's greatest weakness, and he was having trouble being his usual grumpy self. He soaked the ears in butter enough to gag a hog and chomped down double rows of the golden stuff, systematic as a circus crew pounding in tent stakes.

I asked Ma if Mrs. Tobiason kept in touch with her relatives in Sioux Falls.

She glanced at me suspiciously and asked why I wanted to know that.

"They tell me Toby, her husband, isn't too cozy with her tribe, say he hates them and it goes both ways."

"That's poppycock. The colonel paid for Tobiason's studio and equipment, for heaven's sake. Why wouldn't he be grateful?"

"Because the colonel came out owning the studio and Toby, just like he owned the Fox Lounge and Felix. The old boy never gave anything away, he just bought everything and everybody."

Elihu lowered a stripped cob to his plate and grinned at Ma. "I told you that years ago."

"I didn't believe it then," said Ma, "and I don't believe it now. But even if it's true, it doesn't make him a monster. He was just smarter than anyone else. Naturally he wanted to keep things under control. After all, it was his money."

"Was it really?" I asked. "I've never heard a thing about where he got his stake to go into business in Corden. Where'd all his boodle come from?"

"Probably got it from the devil," said Elihu. "Sold his soul for it."

Ma told him to take some more corn and be still. He grinned and returned to gobbling.

When I figured she'd calmed some, I asked Ma how Mrs. Tobiason handled her family relations.

"Wilhelmina handles all her relationships like a lady."

"I guess if she can handle a name like that, she can manage most anything. Who's she close to?"

Ma chose to ignore my question and asked her own.

"Who've you been talking to?"

"Lots. I'm stuck with this problem of how Colonel Cutter showed up in town rich, after he staked a claim and lost two crops in a row."

"Well, contrary to those stories you've been digging through garbage for, I have it on good authority that Colonel Cutter's father was an important man in the East."

"What's this authority claim made him important?"

"Well, he was into politics—a lieutenant governor, I believe."

Elihu took a break from gobbling corn and snorted.

"Lieutenant governors are about as important as horse-apple rollers."

Margaret looked bewildered, so I explained that horse-apple rollers were street sweepers.

Then I folded my napkin and left.

It was only two and a half blocks up to the Tobiason house, and my knock was answered quick as an echo by a young lady who gave me a look that suggested they only made hand-outs at the back door. Her hair was light brown, in soft waves that reached her shoulders; her blue eyes were clear as the South Dakota sky. Ma would think the mouth too rich to be decent and the coloring of her cheeks too bright for innocence.

I asked for Mr. Tobiason.

"Why?" she asked The voice was schoolteacher firm.

"I'm Carl Wilcox. I'd like to talk with him."

"I know perfectly well who you are; what is it you want?"

"To talk about murder. He might be interested."

Her brushed eyebrows rose. She said wait, and went back down the hall.

I sat on the stoop, rolled a cigarette, and was a few puffs into it before the man appeared in the doorway.

He didn't look much beyond the mid-fifties, but his dense hair was white as a biblical patriarch's, and combed and brushed neater than a show dog coat. Made me think of a clean-shaven Robert E. Lee.

"Sorry to keep you waiting," he said in a voice suited to an undertaker. "Please come in."

We moved to the semi-darkness of his living room. All the shades were drawn except on the north, where two small windows admitted light enough to keep me from stumbling over a footstool as I waded through the carpet to the couch and sat while he settled into an armchair to my left and folded his white hands over his small paunch.

"I take it from your remarks to my daughter that you're investigating the Lilybell Fox murder."

I nodded.

"I didn't do it," he said solemnly, and then smiled. It was the frostiest smile I've seen and gave me a hint as to why his wife's family wasn't crazy about him. He made you feel that contempt was something too cozy and intimate to express his low opinion of the world.

"I'll make a note of that. It gives us something in common. Actually, I'm here to talk about something else you might be interested in."

His eyebrows were lots bushier than his daughter's, and raising them took more effort and made more of his attitude.

"Neither of us," I said, "is popular with the Cutters or the Fox clan, excepting your wife, of course."

"What're you getting at?"

"I think Lilybell hated the family even more than you do, and that she had a notion of something smelly about how the colonel got rich, stayed rich, and passed everything on to Wayne. Shirttail relatives have tried to scare me out of poking around, which makes me think there's a reason why they're touchy about anybody poking into the clan's history."

The frosty smile began to thaw. He looked almost friendly.

"And you think I might know something to reinforce this theory?"

"I thought you might like to talk about it."

"Mr. Wilcox, I'm not just interested, I'm fascinated. For years I've known the colonel was a total scoundrel, and I've been certain his descendants were stigmatized by his actions and style."

"Excepting your wife."

"But of course." He laughed. "How delightful. Would you care for a drink?"

We had Irish whiskey and water. He actually got up and

brought it to us from the kitchen, handed mine over with something close to a gleeful grin, and settled back after we'd taken cigars from his case and lit them up. These weren't La Fendrich's or White Owls but genuine Coronas.

"You know Wilda Mahon?" I asked.

"Indeed. The widow who was a combination daughter and factotum in the colonel's household for over a decade. Always suspected the old man tupped her regular. I imagine that's why Wayne suddenly shipped her off to a hovel somewhere remote when he took over management of the family during the colonel's dotage."

"She told me the colonel turned lovey and she went along, figuring she owed him. By the time Wayne offered her the house in Fulton, she was ready because she didn't want to be nursing a senile old man."

"Wilda was always a survivor," he said, nodding.

"My ma claims the colonel's money came from his father, who was supposed to be somebody important in politics back East."

"That's hogwash. His father came to the New World to escape conviction as a thief, bribed his way aboard the ship he sailed on, and arrived penniless."

"Your wife tell you that?"

"Not on your tintype. I learned enough from her to get a few names and wrote some letters to people my father had been close to in Boston, where the first Cutter in America lived."

"Ever tell anyone?"

"No. At best it would embarrass that ass Wayne, but merely exposing the colonel as a liar wouldn't gain me anything useful. I carried out my little investigation for nothing but my personal amusement."

"Ever find out where the colonel's pot actually did come from?"

"No. I'm just certain it didn't come from his father."

"I hear the colonel financed your photography business."

"Did Wilda tell you that? Amazing. You must have quite a talent for extracting information. I've never heard she was a gossip. Well, it doesn't matter, that's the common notion around here. The fact is, Colonel Cutter made no donations to me or anyone else. The Tobiason Studio is a business corporation, originally owned by the colonel, later willed to Wayne. I'm an employee, earning a percentage. It's paid off royally for the Cutter clan. Something like a third of my gross income still goes to Wayne. The colonel never did anything that didn't bring him a generous return. Of course, no one outside the immediate family knows this. It amused the colonel to have people think of him as the open-handed benefactor, and I was too proud to admit I was so short on cash I accepted the deal he offered."

"How'd the colonel die?"

He grinned much as he had earlier. "In bed. Men like the colonel never get murdered. Of course, if wishes came true, you could say it was my doing, but it wouldn't have taken so long if I'd had any real influence. That doesn't keep me from wishing Wayne ill."

"Do you know Uriah Hack?"

"Only by reputation. Some sort of a third cousin to Cole Fox, I believe. There are lots of stories about him. A very bad piece, evidently."

"Know any of the family close to him?"

"Well, there's Tiny Fox. I heard they were pals once. Don't know if they've stayed in touch since Uriah went to the Cities. I hear you've met Tiny."

"Who passed that on?"

"My wife. Someone called her about it."

"Is your wife at home?"

"Yes. Upstairs in her room. You want to talk with her?"

I did.

15

WILHELMINA'S BODY WAS as shapely as a plump pillow. Her face, with its slightly hooked nose, beetled brows, and dark, piercing eyes, gave her the look of a friendly witch, except her lips were soft and full, framing white teeth as she smiled at me from her rocking chair beside the east window. She had looked up from a book in her lap when her husband introduced me. Now she apologetically suggested I sit on the bed, since there was no other chair in the room, thanked her husband for bringing me up, and paid him no attention as he drifted out.

"Every time I recall hearing about Carl Wilcox, from the time you were five, it seemed you were up to some sort of mischief, or involved in some fantastic practical joke. It's hard to believe you've survived all your escapades. Have you ever known peaceful times?"

"It was pretty quiet at Stillwater."

"That's where you served a year in prison, wasn't it?"

"Uh-huh. You mind I ask a couple questions?"

"Well now, that'll depend on the questions."

"Did you know Lilybell Fox?"

"Mostly by reputation. We never lived in the same town, you know."

"What'd you hear about her?"

"It depended on who did the talking. Some of the family considered her a strumpet and climber, a few think she was a murderess."

"What do you think?"

"Well, I came to feel rather sorry for her. From all I heard, she was a girl with spirit who, let's face it, made a bad marriage. Felix wasn't faithful, he certainly had no talents as a businessman, and he was only very superficially bright. From all I can gather, Lilybell was clever, bold, and ambitious. And maybe a little too attractive for her own good."

"You don't think she killed Felix?"

"I suspect she wouldn't have gone out of her way to save him, but no, I can't believe she poisoned him or anything like that."

"You think the family's vulnerable enough that if she set out to prove something bad about the colonel, there'd have been a family plot to get rid of her?"

"Well, since she was murdered, and one of the family, however remote, is suspected of doing it, then the notion does seem possible, but I think it unlikely."

"People have been telling me the colonel took advantage of guys like Felix and your husband. Pretended to be the family Santa Claus, while actually screwing every dime out of anybody he could. What do you think of that line?"

"Will you keep it to yourself if I tell you?"

"All I want is to find out why Lilybell got killed, and then get whoever did it."

"What I tell you mayn't help a whit, but I'm bound to put you straight. Colonel Cutter was a brilliant businessman. Felix was simply a fellow with charm and blarney, but if he'd

been the owner of the lounge, he'd have given it away to his boozing pals. My husband is a wonderful photographer, and he wouldn't give away so much as a smile, but on his own he would never have managed to promote his business into anything profitable, because he has no talent beyond the camera and the darkroom. The colonel got him into doing class portraits, wedding receptions, and all the other things that made money enough to run a profitable studio in a pitifully small town. The colonel saw to it that books were kept for the lounge and kept a tight rein on Felix's partying. Felix and Toby resented him, and they absolutely hated Wayne when he took over. If they'd been honest with themselves and the rest of the family, they'd have given the old man credit for making them both successful. Unfortunately, neither Toby nor Felix have enough wit to recognize, let alone admit, their weaknesses. That's a very common fault of men."

"You know where the colonel got his original stake?"

"No. I can only assume it came during his years in service. He entered the army as a captain and left it a full colonel. Far as I know, he was nearly penniless when he was a captain. Somehow becoming a colonel turned him into a man of means. He never told anyone that I know of how this happened, and if you had known the colonel, you'd realize why nobody would ask him. He wasn't the sort of man people questioned. Not about anything. You accepted him or you stayed out of his way. Since he was always successful and charming, very few people ever crossed him that I know of."

"I guess you admired him."

"A lot of people did. Probably all women."

"You know why Wilda Mahon moved out of the Cutters' home?"

She looked down at the big book she'd closed on her lap when I came in, and for a second was still. Then she lifted the book and asked if I'd read it.

"What is it?"

"*Anthony Adverse.* It's very interesting and popular, but long."

I admitted I'd not read it.

She lowered the book back into her lap and dismissed the subject.

"I'm going to ask you to promise once more that you won't pass on what I tell you—I mean, not as anything I've said."

I agreed.

"It's not a thing I know for an absolute fact, you understand. But I believe Wayne Cutter fell in love with Wilda when he first saw her. You might find that hard to believe, since you never saw her in her prime, but she was something very unusual. There was a certain royalty about her. That sounds ridiculous when you consider she worked for them as a cook and housemaid, but she was able to do it without ever demeaning herself. She was in charge of that house, absolutely. Wilda made you think the work she did was done personally because no one else was capable of doing it properly. Anyway. As the colonel grew old and let Wayne take over the business and the family, he pretty much withdrew to his room, and Wayne saw more and more of Wilda. She fascinated him as she had his father. She was probably no more than ten years his senior, but she cast a spell over him and then wouldn't let him touch her. It made him hate her. When the business came up of this house in Fulton being empty, he got the notion of moving her there. I suspect he was surprised she accepted the idea at once. The old man was opposed, but when she told him she was tired of nursing the whole family he turned sullen and gave her up. I think that killed him. He died within a year after she left."

"She told me she went because she didn't want to nurse a lecherous, senile old man."

"Or to be the mistress of his scheming son."

"She claims Wayne never tried for her—just wanted her out of the house because she was ruining the family reputation."

Wilhelmina thought that was very funny. She laughed so hard she nearly dropped her book, which she finally moved to the floor. Then she groped for and found a hanky in her apron pocket, wiped her eyes, and shook her head.

"If you ever get to the truth of things, you'll probably learn it was her idea for Wayne to give her that house. She's just the sort of schemer who'd realize that'd appeal to him. It was the cheapest way out for Wayne. And probably thought she'd never be able to stand living alone, off in that backwater town, and would come crawling back to him."

"How'd the rest of the family deal with Wilda? How'd they react to the move?"

"She was always an enigma to them. There was never open talk I heard of. I think everyone assumed she slept with the colonel and that Suellen knew it and was content to pretend otherwise. It relieved her of certain obligations she'd never invited or encouraged, and she was so delighted to escape household chores and cooking responsibilities that she wouldn't dream of making a complaint."

"How'd she deal with Wilda's leaving?"

"Wayne handled that very neatly. He hired two women to fill her place, one cook and one housekeeper. Even combined, they couldn't handle the job as well as Wilda, but they were adequate. For all I know, one or both of them serviced the colonel as long as he was able. That's awfully catty, I'll admit, maybe not true. The old man was probably beyond servicing at that point."

"You think they were available to Wayne?"

"Not likely. Wayne wasn't interested in scullery women, which they both were, and Wilda never was. And besides, Doreen was never anything remotely like Suellen. Nobody puts anything past her."

16

I CALLED DAHLBERG, my favorite Aberdeen cop, and told him I wanted to talk with Wayne Cutter about the Lilybell Fox murder.

His comeback was a deep sigh.

"You with me?" I asked.

"The first thing you better get straight," he said, "is you're talking about *Mister* Wayne Cutter. Okay?"

"Yes sir. I'll try to remember."

"It's not like he owns the town. Not all of it. But let's say he carries a lot of weight, okay?"

"You saying I got to get an appointment for sometime next month to check on a murder?"

"I'm saying this's touchier than hell. That's all I'm saying."

"So I'll comb my hair and wear shoes. You want to come along when I look him up?"

"Damned right. You come here, and we'll go over together."

From Corden to Aberdeen isn't more than eighty miles, and you don't exactly strain your eyes on the scenery, so it seems farther, especially in a Model T cruising along at almost forty per. ✓

It was midafternoon when Dahlberg and I walked from the police station to the big man's office on the second floor of a bank building about dead center in the business district. We cooled our heels for twenty minutes in the outer office and finally were led inside, where the Man sat at a desk that wasn't much more than eight feet wide. On the wall behind him was a portrait of Colonel Cutter in the full-dress uniform of the Union army. His hair on top was getting thin, but he made up for it with a mustache that covered his mouth almost to his chin. It looked like he'd have to take all his nourishment through a straw shoved under the brush. It also looked like he wasn't likely to approve of anything anyone in this room could ever do or say.

I examined Mister Wayne Cutter. He still had lots of hair on top, and his face was as smooth as a baby's bottom. There was nothing babyish about his mouth. It had all the softness of an ax blade. His smile didn't improve anything. It surprised me his teeth weren't steel or even pointed.

Dahlberg managed to show respect without being a toady about it, and introduced me in a way that hinted he wasn't really responsible for anything to come.

Cutter's eyes, peering from under dark brows, took me in, and his head bobbed once.

"Let's get to it."

"I'd like to know," I said, "if you have any notion about why your cousin Uriah Hack would stick an ice pick into Lilybell Fox."

"If Uriah actually did it, I suspect he used an ice pick because it's a tool he's familiar with."

I smiled to let him know I could take kidding and ducked my head, granting him the point.

"But why'd he want to murder her?"

"I've no idea. Maybe she wouldn't lay down when he wanted

to try her out. You have any sort of proof he actually stabbed her?"

"All circumstantial. He showed up fifteen minutes after she arrived in town, was upstairs during the first part of the night after she'd gone up to bed, and left the hotel in the night without paying his respects or the room bill."

"So, at the very least, you want to find him and collect that bill?"

"At the very least."

"Did he sleep in the bed?"

"Can't be sure. It was opened but unwrinkled."

"Perhaps if he didn't sleep there, he didn't feel any obligation to pay."

"He contracted for it when he signed in. If he didn't like it, he should have come down and checked out, and that would've settled it."

"I don't suppose it would relieve your mind if I simply paid for the night's lodging?"

"Only if we could settle the murder count that easy."

"All right, just what do you expect from me?"

"Your know what Uriah Hack does for a living?"

"The last I heard, he was a repo man."

"What's that?"

"Repossession. One of those fellows who come around to collect for encyclopedias people sign for but don't get around to paying for after delivery. Deadbeats, you know?"

"You think Lilybell bought a set?"

"If she had, I doubt he'd have stabbed her for failure to honor the agreement."

"Who does he work for?"

"I haven't the slightest idea. I'm not my cousin's keeper."

"I talked with Lilybell the night before her murder. She told me she was checking out your family history. That she suspected there was something fishy about your father's money—figured it came from shady dealings before he showed up in South Dakota. Some people I've talked with think she was killed to stop her poking into the record."

"I see. I'm to explain where our fortune came from or be suspect, is that it?"

"Any reason you wouldn't want to tell us where his money came from?"

"None. Absolutely none. I simply don't know for certain. The colonel was not a man you questioned on such matters. I never dreamed of asking. I do know that he was the sort of man who inspired confidence in anyone who dealt with him. I've no doubt that he could always obtain loans for whatever enterprises he launched. It didn't occur to me to poke into the details."

"Know where Uriah lives?"

"No. I suspect his is rather a gypsy life. The last we heard, he was working out of the Twin Cities area. The truth is, the whereabouts and career of Uriah Hack have never been a big item in my life."

"Does he come from your side of the family, or your wife's?"

"Hers."

"Would we find her at home?"

He gave me his sharp steel smile.

"Not likely. She might be with her bridge group, or at the church, or shopping. Doreen's not a homebody."

"Any objection to my talking with her?"

"None. And I wish you luck in finding her. Now, if you don't mind, I've a business to run."

Back at the station Dahlberg looked up the Cutter's home telephone number, and I made the call.

The voice that answered was soft as a kitten's purr. I explained who I was and where I was calling from and asked if we could drop by for a few minutes.

She said of course.

We got the address from the telephone book, climbed into Dahlberg's car, and drove over.

17

WAYNE CUTTER'S HOUSE wasn't as big as a cathedral and had no stained glass windows, but it was still grand enough to make an ambitious woman like Ma drop to her puritanical knees in awe. Poking the button at the entrance didn't cause a distant buzz or ringing, it set off chimes.

I expected at least a uniformed butler, but instead a young woman wearing a sullen frown, a pale blue housedress, and high-heeled shoes appeared and looked us over with distaste.

I identified my partner and me and said Mrs. Cutter was expecting us.

That brought a smug grin. "Oh yes, Mrs. Cutter got a call right after yours and had to leave. A family emergency. She said to tell you she was very sorry."

"Say when she'd be back?"

"No. One can hardly schedule emergencies, can one?" She really enjoyed sarcasm; it made her glow.

"Where'd she go?"

"I'm sure I don't know. She didn't tell me, and I wouldn't ask her, now would I?"

"You her daughter?"

"I am," she said, drawing up a bit. "How'd you guess?"

"You look too smart to be a maid. How many kids in the family?"

Her eyes narrowed suspiciously, but my examination of her face seemed to reassure her, and she suddenly tilted her head and grinned again.

"There's me, my sister, and two brothers. Why do you ask?"

"I thought if there were too many, maybe I could adopt one of the tribe to keep the place from being too crowded."

"Go on, you don't look like you could adopt a cat. And I'll bet this is the biggest house you've ever seen."

"I've seen a place in France with closets bigger than this whole joint."

Her eyebrows elevated. "You've been to France? Oh, sure, in the war."

"Well, shucks, I'd hoped you think I went as a tourist. You're too fast for me. So what really happened? Did your dad call and tell your mother to scat?"

She frowned. "I don't know who called, that's the truth. Mom answered the phone, listened, said all right, told me she had to run and I was to apologize to you and say there was an emergency."

"Did she look worried?"

"Mom wouldn't look worried if she woke and found her bed on fire."

"So who in the family might have an emergency?"

"Any of them. And we're not just talking about sons and daughters. Mom takes care of the whole crazy clan when they ask—and most of them do, often."

"Which way did she go?"

"I was in the kitchen when she told me, and she went out the front door. I've no idea which way. And wherever she went, she wouldn't want strangers hounding her when she already had a problem to handle, so just forget her today. Okay?"

By this time she was enjoying the game, and she asked if we'd like some coffee. I was dumb enough to agree, thinking I could pump her, but it turned out she was even smarter than I'd figured on first sight. We got nowhere. She even tried to make me talk about myself, and if Dahlberg hadn't been around, I'd have gone into it. She ignored him, admired my cigarette-rolling technique, and poured coffee until we retreated before it became necessary for us to use their bathroom.

"What do you think?" I asked Dahlberg as we headed back to the station.

"I think you might be able to get someplace there if you were good-looking, ten years younger, and owned a bank."

"I was thinking about where the mother went—and why."

"You were thinking about getting laid."

"Not a bit. Well, not much. You think Wayne called and told his wife to scram?"

"I figure she's probably up in her bedroom, laughing at us."

We parked in front of the station and slouched in our seats, watching the sunbaked street, the rare auto traffic, and a few pedestrians.

"What do you know about Mrs. Cutter?" I asked.

"She's queen mother of the clan. Went to nursing school back east when she was fresh out of high school. Met Wayne when he got his appendix out and spent a week in the hospital. She's got more go than a kennel full of pups and generally rules the roost, right down to fourth cousins. Some folks think Wayne's no more than her top manager as far as even his businesses are concerned."

"What do you think?"

"They're a team. Between them, they're about the equal of the colonel himself in his prime."

"I've got to talk with her."

"Lots of luck."

I figured it would take more than that.

18

AFTER SPLITTING FROM Dahlberg I found a cheap hotel and got settled in. The next morning I went down to the phone booth to call Wayne Cutter's number. The only useful information Doreen Cutter's daughter had turned over was her own name, Giselle, and I recognized her voice the moment she answered.

My line was short.

"Dahlberg, the Aberdeen cop with me yesterday, says you wouldn't give me a date unless I was better looking, younger, and owned a bank. Is he right?"

"It's not likely I'd marry you, but I'm not that fussy about dates. What've you got in mind?"

"Is there a movie on you'd like to see tonight?"

"I've already got a date for the dance. Tell you what—why don't you come around, and I'll promise you a dance and stretch it some if we get along."

That sounded like a great runaround, but it wouldn't be my first, so I said sure and asked for directions to the dance hall.

She supplied that and said she'd probably show up a little after nine.

The hall was already crowded when I drifted in at nine-fifteen and spotted the familiar bandleader, old Hollering Holly Horn, up on the bandstand. He was probably the hottest music man in South Dakota in those years, but it had never made him snooty toward old friends. He returned my wave with a wink and a grin.

I stood with the stags along the north wall and took in the girls, mostly sitting on folding chairs along the west side. The band was playing a slow one, and dancers were snuggling or dreaming as they shuffled around the waxed floor.

Giselle entered with her date and another couple at nine-thirty. Her partner was nearly a head taller than me and wore a suit worth more than all the clothes I've ever owned, maybe excepting boots. The other girl looked like she might be Giselle's sister. She had the same face, only it was rounder, and her blond hair was cut in a bob. Giselle's hair floated down to her shoulders. The sister's date was hefty and big-jawed, with a friendly grin. Giselle spotted me at once and tipped her head back in greeting. Her smile was a little too wide and warm, and her boyfriend caught it and glowered around, trying to see the target. His eyes passed over me as if I didn't exist, then snapped back when he found no other likely prospect.

He bent over her, and there was a short argument, which ended when Giselle led her group over and introduced me. The girl was Edyth, her younger sister. The tall dude was Wendell Ecke, and I didn't catch the other guy's name.

"Mr. Wilcox," Giselle told them, "is from Corden, investigating a murder. He thinks it has something to do with our family."

"Like what?" demanded Ecke.

"You really want to know?" I asked.

He glared at me. Tall guys usually think glaring from on high intimidates short people.

"Yeah," he said.

"Fine. Let's go to a café, get a booth, and talk about it."

"We came here to dance," said Edyth. "I'm not going someplace to talk." She looked at her date, who grinned, took her hand, and led her to the floor. Ecke glanced at Giselle, who watched me. He looked back my way.

"You willing to talk?" I asked Giselle.

"Sure, if you can do it while dancing."

"Now?"

"Why not?"

"Now wait a damned minute," objected Ecke. "Who paid for your ticket?"

"If that's your only problem," said Giselle with a sweet smile, "I'll pay you back. You want it right now?"

He spluttered some, shook his head, and glared at me. Before he could do anything foolish, Giselle took my arm and we moved to the dance floor.

She was so light on her feet it almost made a dancer of me, and we moved in the counterclockwise trail of the general crowd, away from onlookers.

"Why're you sore at your date?" I asked.

"He's stupid."

"When'd you find that out?"

"When I told him I was going to dance with you. He got all huffy, so I said, fine, forget our date. He about had a calf over that but finally agreed to come. The moment he saw you weren't very big he was all set to fight until I told him you'd probably knock his block off, since you'd already whipped Tiny Fox."

"Where'd you hear that?"

"Father told us at dinner tonight."

"Was your mother there?"

She grinned and shook her head. "She's out of town."

"Where?"

"What are you trying to find out about our family?"

"Where Colonel Cutter got his first big stake."

"That's no secret. He was a fantastic businessman. Half the people in Corden worked for him one way or another. He owned a bank and the flour mill and all kinds of property—"

"But where'd he get the dough for all that? There had to be a starting point."

"He started as a farmer. Had one of the first claims in the territory. He and Victor—"

"Come on, they lost their shirts two years in a row, maybe more. And all of a sudden the colonel's investing in businesses. It doesn't add."

She argued that they'd also had good years—I had the story all messed up—but what business was it of mine anyway? Why was I poking into the family affairs so far back?

I told her about Lilybell's program in Corden, and that it appeared a cousin had followed her to our town and murdered her the night she arrived.

"Who was that? What cousin?"

"Uriah Hack."

"He lives in the Cities! In Minnesota, for goodness' sake."

"Yeah, well, there are trains, buses, and cars nowadays, Giselle. People can get around pretty quick. Especially when they're offered money to do a job."

"That's ridiculous!"

"Okay, straighten me out. Why else was Lilybell murdered? She wasn't robbed or raped."

"Most likely it was because the Fox crowd thought she murdered her husband. That's none of the Cutters' concern."

The dance number ended, and she stood staring at me while we waited for the band to crank up again. When they did, it was a livelier number, and I got bold enough to try my hitch step. I had to concentrate to bring it off, and we didn't talk. The room was hot enough to make me sweat; as far as I could see, Giselle just glowed. I glanced at the stag line a couple times and saw Ecke glowering at us. We passed near Edyth and her guy once. He took us in, but the sister was in her own world and didn't know if she was on earth or the moon.

During the break after the second number, I asked Giselle why her father told her mother to scram when I was coming over to see her. She denied that was what happened.

"Did she tell you it was him that called?"

"She didn't say, and I didn't ask."

"Giselle, you're better looking than almost anybody around and I'd guess a lot smarter, but you're not a good liar."

"Well, it's hard to take that as an insult when you put it so sweetly, Mr. Wilcox, but why do you say it?"

"If you and your dad were talking enough for you to find out Tiny and I had a run-in, he'd sure as hell have told you other things, and you'd have asked some questions. Like, did he call your mother? Where is she, really?"

"If she were actually hiding from you, why in the world would you think I'd tell you where to find her?"

"What do you figure I'm going to do? Give her the third degree? Pound out a confession? Why the hell's she hiding?"

"If you'd think, just a teensy bit, you might figure out there's no reason in God's world she'd be hiding from anybody. She went to help one of our relatives, and she doesn't want to be bothered by you or anyone else 'til that's taken care of."

That's all I could get.

We went back to the stag line, and I gave her up to her glowering partner, nodded good night, and left the hall.

Dahlberg approached me as I came out on the sidewalk and asked where I was heading.

"Back to the hotel."

"Get anything from Giselle?"

"Had a nice dance."

"I got some news," he said.

"As the elephant kid said, I'm all ears."

"We just got word a bit ago that Uriah Hack's been murdered. Body was found in a dumpground near Gantry. That's a jerkwater town just fifteen miles southeast of here."

19

THE BODY HAD been identified by the contents of a wallet in his back pocket, Dahlberg said. The man's face had been wiped away by buckshot, so there was some suspicion the wallet was a plant.

I returned to the dance hall and found Giselle standing by Ecke, not listening, while he jawed at her. She spotted me at once and watched my approach, frowning. Ecke turned and glared.

"Uriah Hack's turned up dead in a small-town dump," I told her. "Face blown away. Do you know a guy named Jim Olson? Young, narrow nose, wide nostrils, heavy eyebrows. A little bowlegged?"

She shook her head quickly. "What's he got to do with anything?"

"He checked into the hotel the night Lilybell and Uriah showed up. He paid in advance, was gone in the morning."

"How was Uriah killed?"

"Shotgun, I guess."

She took a deep breath and said, "I'm going home. Walk me, all right?"

"You think your mother'll talk with me now?"

"We'll see."

"What the hell," demanded Ecke. "What about me?"

"Nothing about you," she said. "This is family, it doesn't concern you."

He argued that it shouldn't concern me either. She told him he was being childish, and we walked out. He trailed along, still protesting, until she halted on the walk, faced him, and glared until he shut up.

"Go home," she said. "Leave me alone for now—understand? If you want, call tomorrow, but tonight forget about me. I've more important things worrying me right now than your precious ego."

The walk was only four blocks, and she wasn't in a talking mood, so it was done in total silence. She led me into their living room, said wait, and went upstairs. There was some faint murmuring for a while, then two pairs of footsteps sounded along the upper hall and down to the living room.

Doreen Cutter was shorter and rounder than her daughter, but moved lightly on small feet and took me in with solemn, bright blue eyes. Her smooth cheeks were carefully rouged and lightly powdered. She stopped in the center of the room as I stood up to meet her.

"I must apologize for walking out after agreeing to meet you here, but there actually was a call for my help, and family always comes first. Would you care for coffee?"

"No thanks, just some answers."

We sat down with the two women facing me.

"Where's your husband?"

"At the neighbors'," she said. "Playing cribbage. It's become something of a Saturday-night ritual."

"Why'd you decide to talk with me?"

"Giselle tells me there's been another murder. She's been quite impressed by you, and I've agreed we have to face this horrible business. I'll try to be as helpful as I can."

"Okay, from what I've heard, Uriah wasn't exactly a family favorite, but since they heard he's dead, they seem to feel different. Why'd that change the picture?"

She lifted her hands, then dropped them in her lap.

"It wipes out simple explanations for Lilybell's murder. Frankly, we had presumed Uriah stabbed her when we first heard about it all. Felix was the one member of the family who'd been sympathetic toward Uriah. He even arranged for him to get the job he's had for the last couple of years. It'd be entirely in character for Uriah to believe rumors that she'd murdered Felix, and try to avenge him. But this new murder changes everything. I can't imagine what to make of it. Are you certain it wasn't suicide?"

"The cops don't seem to think so, but they're still checking."

I gave her Ma's description of the man who signed in as Jim Olson, including the clothes, and asked if it sounded like anyone familiar. She stared at me a moment, then shook her head firmly.

"It doesn't happen to match one of your sons, does it?" I asked.

"It falls far short of a portrait. Anyway, my sons are out of town just now. Both of them."

She expected me to probe that. I switched my line.

"How'd Colonel Cutter and Cole Fox get their stake to start a business here?"

She visibly relaxed and managed a patient smile. "It was very simple, Mr. Wilcox. You didn't need a fortune to start a business in South Dakota in those days. People didn't suddenly buy into established companies and expand them, they started at the bottom in towns where people were moving in by the hundreds with endless needs and wants. Farmers didn't go deep in debt, they lived off the land, scraped and scrimped, suffered and dug out. Victor, by staying on the farm, was able to feed his brother and wife and his own family in the hardest times, while the colonel started the grain mill and then got into banking. In those days, everyone worked together for the common good. They were happy to follow and help a man who knew what was needed and how to provide it. The colonel had a genius for organization and for dealing with people."

"How close were the Cutter brothers just before Victor died in the blizzard?"

She examined me for a moment, trying to guess what I'd dug up already, and evidently decided nothing was more disarming than a little honesty.

"Well, I'm sure it's common knowledge that they weren't getting along as well as in the earlier days. Victor became resentful of his brother's great success and couldn't hide it. He also began drinking heavily, which offended the colonel deeply."

"I hear Vic beat his wife."

"I suspect that's been exaggerated, but I must admit it was common knowledge that drink made him moody and even mean, occasionally."

"Was the real trouble because Victor's wife got pregnant by the colonel?"

She flushed. "You *have* been picking up all the nasty gossip, haven't you? I suggest you consider the circumstances; how in the world would the colonel find a way to make love to a farmer's wife who almost never left the claim?"

"Farmers spend hours a day working fields a good ways from the house. A man like the colonel can come and go when and where he likes. And he left all he had to Wayne, his so-called nephew."

"Who else would he leave it to? The colonel was childless and took responsibility for his brother's son and daughter when Victor died. He made Wayne his heir, knowing he'd take care of his sister and Suellen."

"Who'll take over from Wayne?"

"Probably Sigmund, our older boy. It's early to say, he's just finished college. Gunnar's just finished high school. There's plenty of time to settle things after Wayne retires."

"What's the young brother like?"

"He's bright, a good student, and very mature."

"How about Sigmund?"

"Very much the same."

"They close?"

"They have been. Since Sigmund went off to college they've not seen that much of each other, but they still get on well, I'm sure."

"I'd like to talk with Gunnar."

"As I told you, he's not home this week. Visiting a friend out East—New York State, I believe."

"Got the address?"

She laughed easily. "How embarrassing. Actually, I don't. He was supposed to write and give it to me, but hasn't gotten around to it yet. I'm afraid he's not a diligent correspondent."

"How about Sigmund?"

"They're together."

I looked at her long enough to embarrass a thin-skinned type, but she only gazed back with a faint smile that lingered through my good-bye.

Giselle stayed with me out to the sidewalk and took my arm.

"Tell the truth," she said. "You tricked her into admitting there was trouble between Victor and the colonel before Victor's death, didn't you? You hadn't really heard any such gossip."

"It seemed likely, so I tried it."

"What of it? What difference would it make?"

"Well, that's just one of the things that's got to be sorted out. Thanks for your help. You'll hear from me."

20

BACK IN CORDEN Sunday morning, Joey agreed to call on store owners in their homes around town, asking if they had seen Jim Olson. We covered everything from the café and pool hall to bakeries and butcher shops. The last place I thought of was the movie theater. We talked with Becky Lundstrom, the ticket seller, and yes, she'd seen a young fellow who answered my description. He came in right after the feature started and bought a box of popcorn.

Asked if she noticed anything unusual about him, she said only that he hadn't seemed in any big hurry to get inside, even though she'd warned him the show had already begun. Mostly he had been interested in getting plenty of butter on his popcorn.

Later, sitting in the hotel kitchen over coffee, I told Joey the only move left was a trip to Sioux Falls for a talk with Tiny Fox.

He peered at me with his melancholy eyes and said that could cost money, time, and maybe my neck.

'Yeah. That's why you better figure a way to get a cop

there to keep me company for the Fox meeting. And make damned sure this cop isn't one of the clan."

He pointed out that he had about as much influence on Sioux Falls cops as I'd have with the pope, and besides, it was Sunday and there'd be nobody around to talk to who had any pull.

By Monday morning I figured another angle and borrowed Joey's telephone to call Lieutenant Baker in Aquatown. Joey said that was a good idea, since Baker was now the chief of police. I made the call.

Baker accepted my congratulations with suspicion and admitted reluctantly that he knew his counterpart in Sioux Falls. My request for help didn't bring his usual resistance. Evidently he figured no one would hold him responsible for my actions. He agreed to call the chief there and told me to call him back in the afternoon.

Baker must have enjoyed the talk with the Sioux Falls chief. He was in a great mood when he answered his phone.

"He says come ahead," said Baker. "Drop by the station and ask for Sergeant Ahern. He's the chief's pet on the force and knows the Foxes well. He'll take you around to see Tiny."

He went on to warn me against getting pushy or wise. I'd better pay damned close attention to my escort's advice, and move careful as a rat in a fox den. "You go messing around on your own and you'll wind up hamburger quicker'n a cat can lick her ass."

I thanked him as humbly as I'm able, dealing with a man so interested in animal life, and said I owed him one. He assured me that knowing that would be a source of great comfort all his days. He put enough sarcasm into it to make me feel I owed him more than a favor.

Ma was stoical about my travel plans, as usual. Margaret didn't seem exactly heartbroken about me leaving either, which, remembering her enthusiasm on the couch so recently, was a letdown.

Sioux Falls is well south of Corden but doesn't quite reach palm tree territory, and the scenery is fine if you like looking far and seeing only sky and prairie with few distractions beyond fence posts, telephone poles, windmills, decrepit farmhouses, corn cribs, and tall gray silos. Once in a while I traded stares with skinny, glum cattle by fences along the graveled road.

Sergeant Ahern was a surprise. Baker's report that the guy was the chief's pet made me expect a spit-and-polish type; this bird was strictly old shoe. He was too big for his uniform, which had more wrinkles than a mummy; his cheeks had the blush of a boozer, his nose was almost as broad as his grin, and the cigar stuffed in the corner of his kisser looked like a permanent fixture.

"Well," he said, "the giant-killer's back. When the Foxes learn of it, they'll be getting up a lynch party."

"You think Tiny'll talk with me?"

"Oh, he and the rest can't wait. They'll be wanting to talk with clubs and knuckles, I'd guess. You know Tiny's on crutches?"

"That ought to slow him some."

"It has. But the others you knocked about are all well and eager."

"How do we go about this?"

"Why, you just tag along with old Sergeant Ahern and you'll make out fine. With luck."

Tiny ran an auto and general repair shop. The building didn't look more than twenty years old, but it had been thrown together like a lean-to and didn't seem strong enough to survive the prairie winds and snow come winter.

We walked through open double doors in front and turned left into the shop office, where Tiny sat at a cluttered desk. His crutches leaned against the wall behind his chair.

Even sitting he looked monstrous, but his expression was

a total switch from what I'd looked up at as he stood over me
in the café before. It didn't seem possible, but there was a
thoughtful look in the dalmatian eyes.

"I don't guess you two have formally met," said Ahern
with what, for him, was a straight face. "This here's Carl
Wilcox, from Corden. Carl, meet Tiny Fox."

I stepped up to the desk and stuck out my hand, half
expecting to get jerked across the desk. He calmly reached
up, and we shook. He didn't even try to crush my knuckles.

Sergeant Ahern kept talking.

"Like I told you when I called to say we were coming over,
Carl knows you and Uriah were cousins and figures that since
Uriah's been murdered, you might like to help him find out who
did it, in spite of the little spat you two had not long ago."

So now I knew why I hadn't been jerked across the desk
and why this guy's eyes were thoughtful instead of murderous.

"Sit down," said Tiny.

We took straight-backed chairs facing him.

"What do you want from me?"

I described the man calling himself Jim Olson, and told
of his checking into the hotel the same night Uriah and Lilybell were there. Tiny scowled and said my description wasn't
enough to help any, he'd need more.

"Right now, that's all we've got. Never saw the guy myself. My ma did. Joey, Corden's cop, has checked all over
town, but the only lead we got was from the ticket seller at
the movie theater. She says a guy like that came into the show
and bought popcorn, and he didn't seem awful excited about
catching the show. But that's it. Nobody else admits seeing
him. It's maybe far-fetched, but it looks like this bird was
tailing Lilybell, found her stabbed, figured Uriah did it, went
after him, and killed him. If that's what happened, the killer
must be familiar with the whole family and Uriah's rep, and
I thought you might know him."

"I don't. And you don't know Uriah killed the woman."

"That's right. So if this Olson guy did it, he still must've done Uriah. Which is a good reason for you to tell us something you know or can figure out about why."

Ahern leaned forward.

"How serious you think any of your family was about the notion Lilybell killed Felix?"

Tiny rubbed his broad chin, then shook his head. "It was talked about, but nobody took it serious enough to kill the dumb bitch."

"Why'd you try to buffalo Carl at the café?"

"Took him for a wise guy trying to stir up stuff about our family. Seemed like a good idea to run him out."

"That's it? Pardon me, old friend, but that doesn't wash, you know? Here's Wilcox in town, trying to find out why a woman got murdered in his hotel. You've heard of him, don't tell me you haven't. It's not like he was some nosy hick poking around. He comes into where you're having lunch, and you get up and tell him to make himself scarce. What were you afraid he might dig up?"

"I figured he'd find out Uriah'd been buddies with Felix, and he'd get the notion the killing was Uriah's work, because of stories around how this twitchy got it with an ice pick."

"So you're willing to talk now, because of Uriah's murder?"

"That's right."

"Ever hear Lilybell had a fella or two?" I asked.

He liked the idea, but after a moment, shook his head. "No, I got to admit, I never heard she was messing around. Of course she might've been too cute for us—"

"I hear Colonel Cutter had a hand in most of the businesses run by his family and yours. He help you set up this garage?"

"Not on your life. When you messed with that old bastard,

he always wound up in charge. This here business has been mine from the start."

"How do you get along with Wayne Cutter?"

"We got no truck with each other."

"Ever hear the story that Wayne might've been the colonel's son, not Victor's?

"Oh hell yes. For some reason all the women went for that old fart. Money, I suppose. Power."

"Anybody still alive around here that served with the colonel during the war?"

"There's old Woody Woodford. He was the colonel's orderly when Sherman made his little sashay through Georgia."

"Where'd we find him?"

"Lives with his son's family, someplace on Nesmith Street."

I suggested to Ahern that we take a ride to see the orderly. Tiny wished us luck and almost sounded as if he meant it.

21

A H E R N   A N D   I stopped for supper before driving to the Woodford house.

"Hell," he said, "this Woody must be older than Methuselah. What do you think you're gonna get from him?"

"Some of these old guys that can't remember what they had for lunch today can tell you what cards they held in a poker game fifty years back."

"So? Who can call 'em a liar?"

"We haven't got much else."

"Okay, this is your baby."

I suggested we go in my Model T. The notion amused Ahern, who said, "Why not?" and climbed in beside me. I wished he were a plainclothes cop so we could claim we were just a pair of Civil War nuts looking for dope about his experiences, but we'd have to play it straight and hope he was the type who'll tell all they know to anybody who'll stay half awake.

The Woodford house was a two-story square job, facing south, with a porch across the front and around both sides.

Scrawny lilac bushes flanked the sidewalk up to the front stoop, and a row of elms grew along the southern lot border, shading the house.

The woman who answered Ahern's knock had thin gray hair pulled tight in a bun, gray eyes bulging behind steel-rimmed glasses, and a mouth all wrinkled tight. She looked old enough to be Abe Lincoln's widow, and I asked if she was Woodford's wife. She informed me icily that she was his daughter. My quick claim that I'd heard he'd married a young one didn't sell, but when I explained we wanted to talk with Woody about his Civil War experiences, she turned from sour to sweet and never thought of asking why we wanted to know such stuff.

"He'll be tickled pink," she said. "Loves jawing about the war. It'll put him in a good mood for a week."

The old man, who was standing by the front window when we entered the parlor, moved creakily to an overstuffed chair in the corner as we sat down. His beady brown eyes took us in, alert as a squirrel watching a hawk. His skull was smooth and bare, in contrast with his wrinkled face and bushy white mustache. His eyebrows were thick and straggly.

Before I could start my pitch about us being Civil War buffs, the old man fixed me with a hard stare and said, "I see you're from Corden."

That lifted my eyebrows, which made him grin. He tipped his head toward the window and said he'd spotted my license plate with the Corden number.

I confessed he was right, told him my name, and didn't catch a flicker, so guessed it meant nothing to him. When I introduced Ahern, the old man's grin faded, and his eyes narrowed.

"So what's a cop care about the old war?"

Ahern gave me a look. Abandoning my cagey approach, I told him exactly why we'd come to see him.

The grin returned. He sat down, settled back, and asked just what did I want to hear?

"How long you served the colonel, how he operated, what'd you think of him, and how'd you happen to come here after the war."

"What's all that got to do with your murder?"

"We won't know until you tell us what you can. It's just possible the murdered woman was stabbed because she was poking into the colonel's past and somebody wanted it stopped."

The bright eyes studied me.

"Was your pa in our war?"

I shook my head. "Too young."

"So was I. Didn't keep me out, though. Lied about my age, enlisted back in 1863. I was small, but already shaving regular, and that was enough for the fella at the recruiting station in New York, where I signed up. I'd been in the service three months when the colonel spotted me on a drill field one morning and right off guessed I was too young. He sat me down and made me confess, and then he said, all right, he admired my guts and he'd make me his orderly until I was old enough to fight. He was only a major back then. They made him lieutenant colonel less'n a month later, and in 1886 he got the eagle. Told me half the credit belonged to me, 'cause I kept his uniform in such fine shape and his sword polished so bright. Never saw his beat."

"Liked him, huh?"

"We all did. Every man jack who served under him. The colonel was a leader that led. I mean up front. If you went through shit, he tromped it first, and you didn't care. I saw him cry over dead officers and privates alike, and he wrote letters to widows and kin, letting 'em know what heroes their boys had been. All the colonel's men were heroes. Every blessed one. Officers and privates, it didn't make no difference."

"Did you come west with him directly after the war?"

"Hell yes. He promised me work long as I lived, and I never gave a thought to doing anything else."

"What'd he have you doing first?"

"Staked a claim near here, just west of the colonel's. Wasn't good as his, had a slough along the west side, but it looked good to me. First winter was real tough. Snow up to your ass, colder'n a well digger's ass in Texas. I helped out the colonel and his brother, Vic, trapping and hunting. We made out. They both had wives by then. I was single—hell, I was only nineteen, not old enough to stake my own claim legal, but the colonel, he told me, write 'twenty-one' on a piece of paper, slip it in your shoe, then you can honestly swear you're over twenty-one. He vouched for me, and of course nobody'd argue with him. When I was twenty I started courting one of Cole Fox's nieces, and we got married before I was twenty-one. I was lying about my age then. Bridget, my wife, never did know how old I was. She's long gone."

"How'd the colonel pay for the grain elevator he built in Corden?" I asked.

"On the come, as they say. Bank was happy to give him a loan. Knew he'd be good for it."

"That was before he and Cole started their own bank?"

"Uh-huh. There was no bank in Corden then, he got the loan from folks in Aquatown who got their start from bankers in Minneapolis, I think it was. None of that was any of my business. I just knew everybody who met the colonel could see he was going places and wanted on his bandwagon. I helped Cole manage the grain elevator about five years, and then the colonel backed me in opening my own feed store."

"He owned it and you managed it, right?"

"Sure. Why not? It was his money. Worked out fine for me right up 'til the drouth and bust. When everything went to hell we closed the store and I retired."

"I hear the colonel was quite a one with the ladies."

"They went for him, no mistake. Why not? He was a fine figure of a man, the most successful in the state, naturally they cottoned up to him. But that didn't mean nothing. He never lost his head. Not the colonel."

"We've heard he was Wayne's real father."

He glared at me. "Where'd you hear that blather?"

"Pretty much all around."

He shook his head sorrowfully. "Envy's an awful thing, you know? People jealous, they'll say most anything. Specially to a stranger."

"They say Wayne's a hard man," said Ahern. "Dangerous to make mad."

"Well now, I guess he's some thin-skinned, and he's got a long memory. Happens to a man who takes over from what you could call a hero. Always in competition with the past, you know? Makes some types owly."

"You think he takes after his pa?" I asked.

"Never really knew his pa. Just his uncle. Wayne's no match for his uncle. Folks don't take to him the same way. But he's damn smart about money."

Ahern asked what action Woody had seen with the colonel during the war, and he said they'd been with Sherman in the siege of Atlanta and the march to the sea afterward.

"The Atlanta thing, that was all heat, dust, bugs, and bodies. Chiggers was more trouble than Rebs. Chewed us raw. We found they didn't like salt, and some tried washing with it and water, but there wasn't enough to go around so a few of us lucky ones rubbed down with bacon and that helped.

"We pushed the Rebs out of Dalton, Cassville, and Altoona, but got stalled at Petersburg. That's where old Sheridan ordered the artillery barrage that killed Bishop Polk right before Johnston's eyes. We were lucky, missed out on the Kennesaw Mountain slaughter. They had to call an armistice there to bury bodies 'cause the stink got so bad nobody on either side could breathe. But the siege of Atlanta done them in. We strangled the poor bastards there.

"We were at Cedar Creek when General Early attacked. Old Sheridan was asleep in Winchester at the start of it, and came on the gallop when our lines were falling back. Dear God, but didn't he raise hell! Colonel Cutter tried to tell him how damned glad we were to see him, and he said never mind the goddamned talk, we got to fight, and we did.

"In November Sheridan took Atlanta. You probably heard he burned it, but that town was blazing when we moved in. The Rebs done it to keep us lean. So we moved through the fire and headed for the sea, grabbing everything still standing. It was a hellish mess. The colonel tried to help some folks left behind, and raised hell with troopers that turned too rough with women, kids, and slaves they found. He had a squad of boys kept things in order as much as they could. Even left live chickens and a few cows when they could manage where plantations still had folks hanging on."

Ahern asked what kind of system the colonel had for handling loot picked up at plantations and small towns they occupied. Old Woody stared at him a second, then shook his head.

"The colonel didn't stand for any of that in his sight. Nobody stole stuff on orders anywhere. Sure, it happened, no way anybody can stop that in war. Like there was this one plantation where our boys dug up a dog's grave when they got suspicious of the soft ground and figured they'd find jewelry or silver buried. That happened three days running because each gang coming through dug it up, then buried it before moving on, so's they wouldn't be the only fools around."

He told us more of misery and slaughter than we wanted

to hear, but nothing specific about how the colonel might have profited. If you believed old Wood, the man had a halo.

At ten his daughter came around to say it was time the old man got his rest. He didn't thank her for the interruption, but I was grateful by then, because I'd given up all hope of getting the truth from him.

22

THE HOTEL I stayed in was only a tad classier than the Wilcox in Corden, but the rates were double. The clerk didn't look like one of the Foxes, and neither did anybody else around the lobby. After cold-eyeing me and my ditty bag, the skinny clerk asked for payment in advance. I didn't blame him. In his place I would have done the same.

I propped the room's straight-backed chair under the knob after turning the lock and thought briefly of my vulnerable Model T out front, but didn't stew about it. Since Tiny apparently wasn't going to be a problem, it didn't seem likely his clan would mess with me for a while.

Nobody busted in during the night or intercepted me on my trip to and from the bathroom down the hall. After breakfast in the hotel dining room, I found a phone and asked the operator to ring Woody. The daughter answered, said yes, he was up and about and would be glad to see me again; he'd been talking to some of the Foxes and had questions of his own.

At the house I learned he'd heard of my fracas with Tiny

at the café. It was obvious that, being small himself, the old man was delighted by the notion of a small man whipping a giant. We had to discuss that waltz thoroughly before he'd answer any of my questions. Finally I cut it off and asked if the colonel was already married when he came to South Dakota.

He grinned, showing stained teeth and receding gums.

"Nope. Not him nor his brother Vic. But his sweetie came west in the same wagon with him. So'd Mattie. Both gals filed claims of their own on land connected with the brothers and me. Then they got hitched. Everything perfectly legal and proper."

"What was the colonel's wife's name, and where'd they meet?"

"Suellen. She was a Georgia plantation owner's daughter. Both her and Mattie. The colonel sort of took them under his wing when their old man died."

"Two Rebel daughters went with a Yankee colonel?"

"What the hell, it beat joining up with enlisted men, didn't it?"

"Okay. But there's a little problem here. The war ended in 1865. The colonel and his brother came to this territory in '78. Are you telling me those southern belles hung out with the Cutter brothers for twelve years before marrying them?"

Woody rocked and cackled. "You're pretty cute. But so was the colonel. He put on a little show with an old chaplain friend from the service who went through the motions back in Georgia, so the gals figured they was married all legal and proper. Then he talked them into playing like they were only sweethearts when they come west, so they could stake claims of their own next to his and Wayne's, and after that the wedding was done right here with a real minister and all. Colonel Cutter made sure the claims was filed proper."

Remembering Woody's report of his "over twenty-one"

trick, and the phony first marriage to the rebel daughters, it was plain the colonel's sense of propriety was highly flexible. We were getting along so well I decided not to challenge him on that.

"What'd you do between the war and coming west?"

"Managed the plantation. That was a big mistake. Nothing but grief. No slaves, you know? The colonel stuck it out maybe a couple years, but any way you cut it, we were Yankees in Reb territory, and nobody ever let us forget it. Finally headed west to Missouri. I really went for that. No below-zero weather, lotsa fruit. Stayed there quite a while, but again, it was Rebel country and we was Yanks and the colonel never felt accepted. Finally headed north."

"When'd the colonel give up farming?"

"After the blizzard of '81. He hung on through the crop failures, but that year, the middle of January, we got snowed in and didn't get shoveled out 'til April. No trains or wagons moved in all that time. Drove us nuts, especially the colonel. In May he sold his double claim and mine. We moved to Corden, and he opened a general store. Before long he added a saloon, then went into the grain business, built the elevator, and finally opened the bank. There was no stopping him."

"Was that the saloon Felix took over?"

"Naw. The first one closed with Prohibition. It wasn't 'til '34 the beer parlor got opened. My, how the church folks got up in arms over that! Didn't do 'em a particle of good, though."

"You told us yesterday the colonel got a bank loan to start his business. Now you're saying he had money to start from selling three claims, his two and yours. That wouldn't have come to a hell of a lot."

"Must've misspoke myself. He got enough from the claims to get a start on the general store. That went great, but he had to borrow to build the elevator and start the bank.

Them deals took more money than he had handy. But not just anybody could've scrounged it all up like he did. They gave him money because they knew he'd make out. That's the point."

"How well did you know Lilybell Fox?"

"Not well at all. Knew she was Felix's wife, heard she got fed up with his messing around. There's even some talk she might've done him in."

"You believe it?"

He made a long face that suggested he doubted any woman could kill a real man.

"What did you think of Felix?"

"He was all right. Kinda fella made you think you were doing him a favor coming into his place. When he said, 'How are ya?' you believed he honest-to-God gave a damn. Kinda simple in some ways—or maybe it was the booze made him seem like that sometimes."

"I hear he made out well with the ladies."

"I guess he worked at it pretty hard, and him being a good looker, they came on pretty strong. But he wasn't nothing like the colonel. The difference was, Felix always let 'em know how bad he wanted in their pants. The colonel never let a woman think he needed *her*. The trick was making them think they needed *him*. Makes all the difference, you know? And he was always polite as hell and mostly thoughtful. He could bust up with a gal and make her think he believed he was the loser, but it was for her own good. There's never been anybody to match him."

"When did Cole Fox come in with him?"

"Not long after the colonel quit farming. Cole was smart enough to spot him as a winner the minute he came to town. Right away cozied up."

"Weren't they in the service together?"

"Nah. Cole wasn't never in our outfit or any other that

saw action. Always served somewheres in the rear. Way too cute to get caught up front, where a man could get shot."

"Know anything about Wilda Mahon?"

His grin broadened. "Oh yah. There was a really smart woman. The onliest one too much for Wayne. Hell, in the end, she was too much for the colonel himself."

"How so?"

"Well, she went her own way, didn't she? When he got too old and bothersome, she slickered Wayne into setting her up in that house in Fulton, one of them her husband built before he died. She come off good, believe me. Well fixed. One day, if she takes the notion, she'll go south, just like the robins and geese."

"Did Wayne give her money?"

"Not a nickel. But the colonel left her well fixed. All on his own. She never asked. There's a woman so smart she never had to ask for anything. To keep her, a man had to guess what she wanted, and then add extra. Slick. The colonel appreciated that. Never got over her."

"You admired her."

He laughed. "Admire—that's it. She was way too much for the likes of me."

"Let's go back to the colonel during the war. You guessed, I suppose, that Sergeant Ahern figured the colonel stole a bundle during the campaign years. And nothing you or anybody else has had to say makes a case proving he didn't. It just took too much boodle to manage what the old man built up in Corden, Aberdeen, and Sioux Falls. My guess is the colonel figured it was a sure thing that all those southerners were going to get left nothing and there was no reason why he shouldn't make out, instead of a lot of dumb, grabby sloggers. I think he made deals with plantation owners and businessmen, probably even local politicians. He'd shorten their losses if they cooperated. It just figures that a man who turned out to be such a whiz-bang at big dealing after the war didn't just get smart when he shed the uniform."

Woody gave me his gummy grin.

"You're pretty cagey yourself. Matter of fact, what the colonel done was, he made a few deals to keep Reb sons from being sent back to prisoner-of-war camps. The Reb daddies knew chances were prisoners would die in them camps, so they shelled out big to save their sons. The colonel figured the decent thing to do was help 'em out, and maybe he'd make some friends for the future."

"That story about the colonel picking you out of the ranks, that was phony, wasn't it?"

He chuckled. "How'd you figure?"

"You had too much fun telling it. What really happened? Were you a prisoner of war he rescued?"

"Hell no. My folks didn't have no money to buy me out. We was poor white trash. Daddy was a blacksmith any time he could stay sober. When the Yankees hit Dalton, I was a raggedy kid. Ma, Pa, and me were in the smithy, and it got hit by shellfire. Yankees heard me yelling in the ruins and hauled me out. Ma and Pa both died in it. The colonel come by as they found me, and just took over. Got me a uniform, made me his orderly, and I was his boy ever after. I never looked back. He treated me fine all my life."

"Was Cole maybe one of the Rebel sons the colonel kept out of a prisoner-of-war camp?"

"Nah, I told you straight about him. Yankee all the way. A smart one."

It all figured, more or less. The only trouble was, Woody reminded me of the poker player I'd known some time before; a man who never let the truth spoil a good story.

23

AFTER CHECKING OUT of the hotel I headed for Corden, changed my mind, and swung over to Fulton. It didn't look any better than it had the time before. Wilda answered my knock promptly, smiled as if expecting me, and said come on in.

She offered coffee, but remembering its bitterness I said no thanks. She went to the kitchen after a cup for herself, then joined me in the parlor.

"I presume you've thought of more questions," she said after taking a sip.

"I've been talking with the colonel's old orderly, Woodstock. He claims the colonel's wife was a plantation owner's daughter. So was Vic's wife, her sister, Mattie. How much do you know about all this?"

She stared over the rim of her china cup, then put it down in the saucer on the end table and leaned back.

"Quite a bit, actually. You may find it hard to believe, but Suellen and I were rather close. That's something I don't think even the colonel could understand. She had strong opinions and absolute convictions—despised slavery, not for sentimental reasons but because she felt it corrupted both whites and blacks. She never said as much outright, but I'm certain her father had a black mistress and she considered that hypocritical and unchristian. I think that's what made her contemptuous toward men in general. The one thing she respected about the colonel was that he never pretended to be a faithful, loving husband but stuck to his agreement with her father and provided her with a good home all his life."

"Did the colonel keep Suellen's brothers out of the Yankee prison camp?"

"So I understand. Although no one ever really talked about it. Perhaps they were sent off somewhere in Europe and simply never came back. I don't know."

"I got the notion Mattie never had any children until the Cutter clan came to South Dakota. Is that when the colonel got involved with her?"

Wilda's eyebrows rose a fraction.

"So you figured that out."

"It seemed funny to me she'd be married to a man twelve years before all of a sudden having two kids."

"You're right. I assume Vic was sterile, or impotent. Suellen told me she never slept with the colonel. Not even in the beginning. I don't believe she was in the least bothered by him turning to her sister. She preferred that to him using whores. And she certainly wasn't ever concerned about Victor being betrayed, since he always treated Mattie miserably."

"How well did you know Mattie?"

"Not well. The farm was only a few miles away, but it might as well have been half a continent off as far as I was concerned. We were together on Thanksgivings and Christmases, when she'd work in the kitchen with me. She was prettier than Suellen and didn't talk much. I sometimes suspected she was smarter than she let on; an accommodating woman—pleasant, you could say—but never quite friendly. She seemed to share her sister's views on the war and men, but I never heard her say enough to make me certain of anything about her. The sisters really had no choice in how things went. Their father was broken by the death of one son and the capture of the other two. When Colonel Cutter offered to save the boys from a prisoner-of-war camp, Suellen's father agreed to all the colonel's terms. That included a good deal of gold, and a dowry for the daughters when the colonel promised to marry Suellen and find a mate for Mattie. For all I know, he willed the plantation to the colonel."

"What happened to the parents?"

"I'm not real sure. That's something Suellen didn't care to talk about. I've the impression her mother died shortly after the loss of the first son. Her father probably didn't survive the war long. Certainly he was never mentioned by either of the sisters around me. Neither girl ever impressed me as being a bit sentimental."

"How were things between the colonel and Suellen?"

"Formal. Properly polite at all times. As if they lived by a contract they treated like a religion. I never heard them quarrel. They would argue occasionally, but it never got heated, and they'd simply settle for calm disagreement now and then. Before I arrived they had taken separate bedrooms. For all I know, they may never have shared one. Certainly they didn't after my arrival. Everything was as orderly as a well-run dormitory. They held quiet, very deliberate conferences about the parties they hosted and made careful plans for the education of their nephew and niece."

"And you managed the house completely?"

She smiled again. "Absolutely. Suellen never planned a menu or even how many candles we had at table. She chose party dates, guests, and seating arrangements. The choice of foods was mine, since I knew what I could handle best. I arranged flowers and even picked most of the place settings we used, dishes, silverware, and glassware."

"And you believe her claim that the colonel never slept with her?"

"That's right. He was a very unusual man. Never wanted a woman who didn't want him."

"And you did?"

"Oh yes." She laughed at my expression. "I suppose you've seen that picture of him in Wayne's office. The one where he's all bald head and bushy mustache. It was painted just before he died. When we met, he was much thinner, had more hair on top and less on his lip. But looks had nothing to do with his appeal. One of the things that attracted me to my husband was that he seemed so in charge of his life. He ran a big crew of men with no trouble and was very strong-willed. But compared with the colonel in his prime, my husband was a sweet lap dog. The colonel had a force about him—he seemed in charge of his whole world. That was irresistible to me then. And along with that, he was generous and always seemed so decent. Suellen, I'm sure, rejected him from the start, which only made him indifferent to her as far as sex was concerned. I suppose one of the things I found most admirable in him was his invulnerability. Suellen, I think, appreciated that, but at the same time it probably added to her dislike. None of what made him appealing to others made any impression on her. She is probably the most self-centered woman I ever met."

She went to the kitchen for more coffee, resumed her seat, and frowned thoughtfully.

"Don't misunderstand. Suellen always treated the colonel with respect, in public and in private. She was clever enough to know she had to if he was going to accept their strange life together. She also had enough sense to appreciate that he honored his agreements with her father, married her, and treated her well. And he never had to worry about her getting involved with other men and causing him embarrassment."

"How about women?"

She studied me for a moment.

"Are you asking if she might have been a lesbian?"

"Yeah."

"I don't know. She never did anything to give me that idea, but if she'd been that sort, she was far too smart to be reckless about her own security, and she would never have given the colonel reason to get rid of her."

"How'd she feel about Wayne?"

"When he was little, they were close for a time, much more than she and Iva. But when he grew up and became ambitious, they grew apart, and she never trusted him. After the colonel died, she quietly packed up and moved off to live with Mattie in Minnesota."

"Did Wayne push that?"

"Not obviously. He was probably relieved, but I never heard any talk between them about her plans or his reaction."

"Are Suellen and Mattie still living?"

"Far as I know. In Pine Island. Of course they could have died without my hearing. Never kept in touch."

"You know Wayne's boys?"

"Not really. The older one, Sigmund, went to the University of Minnesota. Graduated this spring. He and his father never got on. The boy loved the colonel, though. Two of a kind, I suspect. The younger brother, Gunnar, graduated from high school this year. When he was little he was fond of me, but I think he heard talk in school that upset him, and he's been very withdrawn the last years. He's a very private boy. A bit moody."

"How'd they get along with their mother, Doreen?"

She laughed. "Everyone gets along with Doreen. She sees to that. A born politician. The perfect wife for a man like Wayne. No temper, no weaknesses, all competence and apparent compassion. She even treated me with tolerance and respect. Mostly tolerance."

I thanked her. She said not to mention it. We walked to the door, and she smiled me out.

24

JOEY WAS IN Eric's Café, stuffing his face with late supper, when I got back to Corden. He listened to the story of my
travels and finally said he guessed next I'd be going to Pine
Island.

"First we got to find out if the sisters are still there."

From his office, he called the Pine Island operator, who
said there was no telephone listing for either woman.

Joey let me call Wayne Cutter's number in Sioux Falls,
and Giselle answered. Yes, both sisters still lived there. They
sent Christmas cards early each December. She found the
address and gave it to me.

"Has Sigmund been home since he graduated?" I asked.

"Oh no. He hasn't been here for over a year."

"How come?"

She sighed. "He and Dad have been at odds for a long
time, but suddenly last year they had a really big blowup.
Sigmund stormed out, and he hasn't been home or written
since."

"Know what it was about?"

"Not really."

"Did it happen right after Lilybell's husband died?"

"Well, yes, I suppose so. Pretty near then."

"Is he sore at his mother too?"

"Must be. He never answers her letters anymore."

"How'd Sigmund know Lilybell?"

"I'm not certain he did. She was in Minneapolis awhile, right after Felix died. If Sigmund knew that, he might have looked her up."

"Why?"

"Well, to see how she was managing. He's a romantic—you know, sort of what you'd call aggressively conscientious. He'd feel an obligation."

"But he feels no obligation toward his parents?"

"No. He only feels for people without power. Know what I mean?"

"I guess so. Does he shut you out too?"

"Pretty much. He's not bitter toward me, at least not the way he is toward Dad, but he thinks I take their side in everything because I haven't left home like him."

She couldn't give me his address or telephone number. It wouldn't make any difference, she said; however mad he was, he certainly hadn't been involved in any murder.

Joey squinted at me when I hung up and asked what'd I been getting at. "You figure this guy Jim Olson is her brother?"

"It seems possible."

"Why?"

"Giselle and her mother, Doreen, seemed a little spooked when I told them about the third hotel guest the night of the murder. It made me think the description fit."

"Come on, you don't figure Wayne Cutter'd use his own son to murder people that gave him some problems?"

"Not if Giselle's right. She says Sigmund hates his father.

It's more likely he'd do anything he could to give him a hard time. All we can do is keep checking angles. Wilda told me Sig took after the colonel. If that's right, maybe Sig's a little nuts about anybody throwing crap the old man's way. He might've wanted to talk with her about the colonel, try to convince her he was really okay."

We walked outside and looked east and west on the highway through town. The only action was bugs haloing the streetlights or crawling around the sidewalks below. The wind wasn't enough to ruffle feathers.

"One of the hardest things to figure," I confessed, "is, if Lilybell died because she was snooping into the colonel's business, why hasn't whoever did it taken a crack at me?"

Joey snorted. "Probably because you're always on the move, or maybe he knows what a tough bastard you are."

"Maybe he just figures killing Lilybell wiped out any chance for me to find out what she was after."

Joey tilted his head for a squint at the sky. All that hard thinking gave him a pained expression.

"That could be it," he decided. "If it was Sig Cutter that killed Uriah because he'd stabbed Lilybell, he wouldn't have any reason to worry about what you might dig up."

"Unless he'd paid Uriah for the ice pick bit, and then figured the guy wasn't smart enough to keep from getting caught and might rat on him."

That was too complicated for Joey, who just shook his head.

THE NEXT MORNING was bright and clear, and promised to be hot. I set off heading east, keeping an eye on the rearview, expecting a tail, but none showed up that didn't pass quick and easy.

It was late afternoon when I hit Pine Island, still well before supper time. I bought gas, got directions to the address Giselle had given me, and moved on. The house was small, set well back on a broad, tired-looking lawn. The porch floor sloped toward the walk, and both steps creaked underfoot. I knocked on the screen door, which still hadn't been changed for winter. It fit badly and rattled.

After a few seconds a figure appeared beyond the inner door's glass, the knob turned hesitantly, and a small, very old party with thin, well-brushed hair peered out at me, breathing harshly.

Smiling my friendliest, I asked which Mrs. Cutter she might be?

"I'm Suellen," she said sharply. "What do you want?"

"Need a little help with a problem involving your family. Could we talk?"

She frowned. "Who are you?"

"Carl Wilcox."

"Ah," she said, with sudden comprehension. "The hobo cop from Corden. You want to ask about Uriah and Lilybell."

"You got it."

She shoved the door open, led the way into her small living room, waved me to an easy chair in the corner, and perched on a sofa to my left. Her eyes, behind wire-rimmed glasses, were bright blue, alert and probing.

"How'd you hear of the killings?" I asked.

"Mary Joe keeps me up to date on the family."

"She used to live in South Dakota?"

"Never. Married a Fox in Rochester. Her husband died, and she moved to Minneapolis but stayed interested in his family. She writes letters like crazy. Probably could write a book on us."

"Is that Mattie I hear in the kitchen?"

"Yes. Why're you here?"

I explained my connection with Joey in Corden and my interest in Lilybell. She took it all in, watching and blinking soberly as I described Lilybell's tale. I asked if it were true that Wilda and she had been friends. She smiled and nodded.

"Did the colonel sell your father's plantation?"

"It was never his to sell. Father willed it to my uncle Burt, who couldn't accept my marriage to a Yankee. Made him frantic. When father died, back in 1868, Burt had us evicted, so we left Georgia and went to Missouri."

"How much money did the colonel get for saving your brothers from a Union prisoner-of-war camp?"

"I never knew. Quite a bit, I imagine."

"Ever hear from your brothers after they were freed?"

"Never."

"You sure they actually got away?"

"No, I'm not. The colonel kept his commitments to my father as far as Mattie and I were concerned. He was childishly fanatical about his honor that way. He liked to believe women were an inferior and helpless lot, and his responsibility. His attitude toward men who couldn't protect themselves and their own was altogether different. I'm certain he was outwardly kind to my father, not because he liked or understood him but because he didn't want to upset me. I had no illusions about how he'd treat my brothers. The truth is, I never cared for either of them. They were selfish drunkards. Only Freddie, who died in battle, was really close to me. He was the oldest of the boys and cared for me like a father."

Catching movement out of the corner of my eye, I turned to see a graying brunette standing in the doorway, looking at me calmly. Her complexion was clear, with tiny creases rather than wrinkles, and she didn't wear glasses. She looked at least twenty years younger than her sister.

"Suellen," she said, "isn't sentimental about anyone. It's

been a great convenience to her. You want to stay for supper?"

I stood as she moved forward and offered a small, cool hand.

"I wouldn't want to be a bother—"

"No bother. I've made beef stew, and there's plenty."

I thanked her, and accepted.

25

WE ATE AT a square table in the center of a kitchen large
as their living room. It was typical of about half the homes I'd
eaten in over the years, except the dishes were fancier and
the flatware was solid silver.

Suellen wanted to know exactly what my authority was
for investigating the Lilybell and Uriah Hack murders.

"None. No badge, no gun, no club or cuffs."

"You just ask questions and bum meals?"

"I didn't ask for a handout."

"But you came right before supper."

"That's when I got to town."

"Convenient. What have you learned about this mess
you're poking into?"

"Not much that's been helpful." I looked at Mattie.
"How'd you like to tell me the real story about Vic's death
during the blizzard?"

She lowered her coffee cup to its saucer, touched her
mouth with her napkin, and looked me in the eye calmly.

"The real story is, he was drunk. As usual. He couldn't

have found the well if he'd been floating in it, but insisted he was capable of going out into a blizzard for water. I told him he wasn't, which guaranteed he'd try. I knew perfectly well, so I suppose you could accuse me of murder. Premeditated."

Suellen shook her head. "Don't pay her any attention. She's always dramatizing things."

"Were you supposed to bang a pan to guide him back?"

"Of course not. In the first place, it was bitterly cold, and the wind was howling like all tortured souls in hell. He couldn't have heard me a dozen steps away from the house if I'd been pounding the pan in the open door while freezing my children."

Suellen scowled at me. "This is all ancient history. What's it got to do with murders now?"

"I never know until I ask. In this case, I about guessed it was like Mattie says. Why'd you let the colonel have the kids?"

Mattie stared at me for a moment. "Because they were his, and he had money."

"How come the colonel didn't offer to take you in along with the kids?"

"He pretended to. And then carefully explained all the reasons why it wouldn't work. With my husband dead, it was just possible there'd be talk if I got pregnant again, and how could he resist me if I were living under his roof? And what do you know, he had an alternative for me in Pine Island, where there were relatives of his partner who'd look after me, and he'd send me a remittance each month and find some employment for me if I wished. He expected begging and tears. He'd have been gently sad and enormously relieved if I'd thoughtfully committed suicide."

"Like I told you," said Suellen, "she has to dramatize everything."

"Did Lilybell know Iva and Wayne came from the colonel?"

"I imagine she heard rumors. But only the colonel, Mattie, and I knew for certain. Naturally there were people who suspected. Some would suspect with or without grounds."

"How about Wayne and Iva?"

"I think they both wondered at times," said Suellen. "Wayne asked me, when he was very young, why the colonel and I had separate rooms. He remembered enough abuse from Vic to hate him and perhaps daydreamed that he'd not been his real father. Iva had no good memories of Vic either and very likely made up her own dreams of who her real father was."

"How about you?" I asked. "Any doubts about who your father was?"

The bright eyes narrowed. "You've been talking with Wilda."

"How'd you guess?"

A few people have been fooled by my innocent act, but neither of these women joined them.

"She raised the same question once. When I told her about my father messing with the colored maid. No, I didn't seriously doubt who my father was, because, even with my imagination, I couldn't picture Mother philandering. God knows, she had plenty of reasons to find love for herself, but she hadn't the gumption, and to be realistic, there simply weren't any handy seducers around when she was young and attractive. I always had to face it, my looks came from father's side of the family. Uncle Bert's older daughter could have been my twin. Mattie, luckily, took after Mother."

Mattie offered apple pie for dessert and even threw in a scoop of vanilla ice cream. Their coffee was the best I'd drunk since Bertha's at the Wilcox Hotel.

It was all so good I wound up feeling cozy and beholden, which made it hard to ask my next questions, but after sitting back and rolling a smoke, I forced myself.

"How well do you know Wayne's boys?"

Suellen smiled at me almost cozily. Mattie looked uncomfortable.

"We've seen little of them," said Suellen. "Used to get together Christmas and Thanksgiving, but haven't now for several years. I understand Sigmund's just finished college and Gunnar's through high school. Both honor students."

"What do they look like?"

"Well, Sigmund's the spitting image of his father. Gunnar takes more after his mother."

"How tall?"

"Both about average—taller than you. I'd guess Sigmund's about an inch more than his little brother, but maybe I think that because he hadn't had time to catch up when we saw him last."

"The mother's Norse, isn't she?"

"Yes, in spite of the English first name, Doreen. How'd you guess?"

"I grew up with Norskies."

"Well, then you know they're not the kind to cause trouble."

"You never know, when the blood gets mixed."

Suellen smiled. Mattie didn't.

"How're things between Wayne and his sons?"

"Wayne and Sigmund haven't gotten along since Sigmund started college," said Mattie. "Maybe before."

Suellen glared at her sister. "What do you know about it?"

"The fact that Sigmund left home as soon as he could and has almost never returned."

"Did he know Lilybell?" I asked.

Suellen shrugged; Mattie frowned, but said nothing.

"Did he ever call you Grandma?" I asked Suellen.

She looked startled, then thoughtful. "Why no, not that I recall—"

"What're you trying to get at?" asked Mattie.

"Whether Sigmund knows who his real grandmother was. What he really thinks of his father, and whether maybe what he suspects made him sympathetic toward Lilybell and mad at his father for not helping her out more when Felix died."

"You'd like to think he's an idealistic young man, set on correcting the wrongs of his father?"

"Either that, or the complete opposite. Maybe he doesn't want anyone to know the facts because he's got big ambitions of his own. They tell me he's a great admirer of the colonel."

"You'll find," said Mattie, icy as a Corden Christmas, "if you really investigate this whole thing, that Sigmund is idealistic, to a fanatical degree."

"Oh Mattie," exclaimed Suellen, "you're being ridiculous. You haven't been around him enough to know a blessed thing."

Mattie made no attempt to defend her opinion. We talked a bit more while I enjoyed a third cup of coffee, but they offered nothing further, and after thanks, I left.

26

I DROVE TO a drugstore, bought a bag of Bull Durham tobacco, got a pocketful of change, found a public phone, called Minneapolis information, and lucked out. The operator gave me a number for Sigmund Cutter.

After several rings a woman answered hello in a voice like somebody expecting great news.

I asked for Cutter.

"Is this Mr. Wilcox?"

"Yeah."

"I'm sorry. He's gone. Why are you looking for him?"

"Is this Mary Jo Fox?"

Her laugh was warm and cozy.

"Yes, aren't you clever? Now I should guess why you're looking for Sigmund. You think he can give you information about Lilybell?"

"I'd like to know where he was when she died."

"Where are you calling from?"

"Pine Island."

"So, you've been talking with the sisters. Well, why don't you come here? We'll talk."

Her voice and style made me forget about trying to pump her by phone. I asked for her address and how late she'd wait.

"If your Model T keeps working, you should be able to make it in a little over two hours. I can stay awake quite a bit beyond that."

She gave me the address, with tips on how to locate it most easily, and I set off.

Mary Jo was a small woman near my age, with inviting brown eyes, freckles scattered across a delicate nose, and a bright grin that made small wrinkles at the corners of her red mouth.

"Want coffee?" she asked as she pushed the screen open and stood aside to let me pass.

"Fine."

I followed her down a straight hall to the kitchen, where she waved me toward a center table and moved to the gas stove for the percolator. The table was set with two white cups on white saucers, a blue sugar bowl, and a matching cream pitcher. She wore a simple black dress with white trim, and no jewelry. Her shoes were black and practical. She poured coffee for us, put the percolator back on the stove, sat down, and smiled.

"How come," I asked, "you're so deep into all the Cutter clan?"

"Because my own family was all too nice and frightfully colorless. Marrying Ian exposed me to endless stories about Colonel Cutter and his family that just enchanted, maybe obsessed me. When Lilybell's husband died, I wrote a condolence letter, she answered, and we began a regular correspondence. She came here during the months she visited Minneapolis as a new widow, and we became dear friends. Felt we should have been classmates."

"So she told you what she was trying to prove about the colonel?"

"The whole story."

"When'd your husband die?"

"Five years ago. Left me with a decent inheritance, lots of time, and loads of family connections. What's your theory about the murders?"

"Let's say I've got an open mind. So far nothing's sure."

"You're trying to sound as if you were quite apart from it all, but I think you went for Lilybell and are hot to catch the killer."

"I liked her, but we hadn't gotten anywhere. She was killed the night we met."

"Ah, you're a romantic."

"Was Sig Cutter living here while he went to the U?"

"That's right. The Fox family is still all involved with the Cutters, and Wayne thought it would be good for Sigmund to have a place to stay where he could sort of keep track of things."

"What'd you do, file reports?"

"Oooh, you can be nasty, can't you? As a matter of fact, he did rather hint that would be appreciated, but I never took him up on it. Do you think Sigmund killed Hack?"

"I want to know where he was at the time Hack died."

"I suppose it would strike you as a young man's kind of murder—especially if he knew, or even suspected, the man had stabbed Lilybell. But Sigmund wouldn't have done it unless he caught Uriah in the act. I suppose almost anyone would have wanted to in his place."

"How well did Sigmund know Lilybell?"

"Fairly well. He met her here, in fact. When she visited me in what must have been his sophomore year."

"Did he know Lilybell was in Corden last week?"

"Yes. He even knew why."

"Did he go there to meet with her?"

"He never told me he was going to. All I know for certain is, he left here last week. I thought he was going back to South Dakota, but I must admit, he was evasive. Now, before you jump to any conclusions, there are a few things you ought to know about him. He's a very serious, conscientious young man, and highly intelligent. He's never approved of his father because of the way he treated Lilybell, Wilda, and even Mattie."

"How was that?"

"He just gave them token support and exiled them from the inner family the moment their men were gone. That kind of cold-bloodedness offended the boy, and I can only admire him for that."

"But it was the old man who sent Mattie to Pine Island."

"Sure but Wayne never made any attempt to bring her back after the colonel died. Never so much as sent her a Christmas card."

"Sig kept in touch with the sisters?"

"Oh yes, faithfully. He's been writing to his grandmother and Wilda since he was in high school. Writing to Lilybell began right after she was widowed."

"When'd he start writing to you?"

She got up, poured us more coffee, and sat down, giving the full wattage of her bright smile.

"When he learned I was studying the family history. He came to see me. We became friends."

"And you're convinced he couldn't have done either of the killings?"

"As I already said, he might have attacked Hack if he saw him in the act, or even if he discovered the body fresh and was able to chase the killer. But it doesn't add up, because Sigmund would never have gone to visit Lilybell carrying a gun, and I can't imagine where he might have picked up one in the Corden area. And it's not in his character to stay in a rage all the time it would take to locate a weapon and run the man down. The only way he could've done it was impulsively, within minutes of discovering the body. Given time, he'd have gone to the police."

"So where is he?"

For the first time she looked genuinely worried.

"If he's not with his parents, I've no idea."

"Maybe they're hiding him."

"That hardly seems likely, if he suspects his father was responsible for Hack killing Lilybell. But who knows? I told you, he's very intelligent, but he's very young too. It isn't out of the question that he'd go home and bring the whole sordid mess to place it in his father's lap. Why don't I go there and talk with them? Wayne knows of my interest, and I don't think he suspects I have anything but respect for the colonel's career and accomplishments. Would you take me there?"

It sounded like the best offer I was likely to get.

27

SINCE IT WAS past midnight by then, Mary Jo suggested we start for Sioux Falls in the morning and offered me Sigmund's room. After giving me a towel and washcloth, she paused at the door.

"Searching the room would be a waste of your time—Sigmund took everything he owned when he left. I checked."

I went to bed only slightly bothered that this woman I'd just met already knew me too well.

She tapped on my door at 7:30 A.M. and served breakfast the minute I reached the kitchen. Her crisp blue dress had white stripes, a high collar, and demurely long sleeves.

As we stowed away scrambled eggs and bacon, I asked what she knew of Gunnar.

"Sigmund's little brother? Not much. Sigmund spoke of him pretty often. Even with four or five years' difference in ages, they were very close. I got the impression they were united against their parents. Once Sigmund left for college, they lost touch some, since Gunnar's not much of a letter writer. That bothered Sigmund a bit."

During our trip to Sioux Falls, Mary Jo said she was writing a history of Corden County that the *Corden Weekly* had agreed to run in a series. What they were paying her didn't amount to much, but it gave her an excuse to keep digging for the local history, which fascinated her.

"The biggest problem is trying to tell an honest story about the Cutter and Fox families. My editor's looking for something that's all puffery for the pioneers and a glorification of their history in South Dakota. When he reads what I've come up with, I suspect he'll either insist on editing it or simply turn it down flat."

"Ever been to Corden?"

"Never. I've a hunch it looks better from a distance, but now I'm heading that way, I'll have to check it all out. There's a limit to what you can learn from letters and libraries."

She had been in touch with old Woody by telephone after learning he never answered letters. He was happy to tell her of the colonel's heroism and qualities as a Yankee officer, but never mentioned his business of "rescuing" captured rebel soldiers for a price, or anything about his techniques for obtaining extra land claims.

After a long, thoughtful silence, she began pumping me for ideas about the case we were following. Among other things, she wanted to know if the destruction of Hack's face didn't make me wonder if the body was really his.

"I mean, maybe the wallet with his picture was planted."

"Yeah, I've thought of that."

She stared hard at me.

"And you're guessing it's Sigmund, aren't you?"

"It wouldn't have to be."

"Don't try to be kind. He's the obvious one." She shook her head. "I just can't accept that. You probably think I'm rationalizing because of my feelings for the boy; maybe you're right. But the notion of a substitute body seems too imaginative for a strikebreaker who kills with an ice pick. Have you talked with the coroner?"

"No."

"I can't get away from my confidence in Sigmund. He's so bright and quick. On the other hand, I can't help worrying—I'm sure he's never had experience with anyone like Uriah Hack. A man like that is too freakish to believe in for anyone as normal, sensible, and young as Sigmund."

She went into a brooding silence until we stopped for lunch in Worthington, and during our meal, she told me she had telephoned Doreen Cutter the night before, right after inviting me to come and visit her in Minneapolis.

"I was pretty frank with her, without ever hinting I was afraid something might've happened to Sigmund. Told her you were coming to see me and that I thought it was important to help you in any way we could. She seemed to agree, but with her you can't quite be sure of anything. I got the feeling she was in control, somehow, that nothing was unknown or even doubtful in her mind. I can't decide whether this is a pose, or means that she will only believe what she wants to. I've about decided she suspects her son killed Hack, or at the very least wanted to, and she'll do anything it takes to keep him from getting caught. If she doesn't actually know anything about all this, she more than likely thinks he hasn't told her anything so nobody can accuse her, or anybody else in the family, of hiding a fugitive."

After a few minutes of silence I asked how come Sigmund had a telephone listing in the directory.

"He had the phone put in during his senior year. Said he'd been using mine more than he felt was proper."

More likely he hadn't wanted her overhearing his calls and contacts.

We reached Sioux Falls by midafternoon, made our first stop at police headquarters, and found Sergeant Ahern.

Mary Jo managed to set aside her fears for Sigmund, pouring on all her charm and warmth to make this cop our buddy. He went to get an extra chair from a partner so we could sit together facing him, and asked what brought the lady to town. She told him quickly and raised the questions we had discussed in the car, without giving a hint of her emotional attachment to Sigmund.

Ahern took it all in, nodding when she expressed doubts about the identity of the latest corpse.

"I've been talking to the coroner. He says the clothes don't fit the body, but other than that, nothing seems especially fishy. They haven't been able to come up with a positive ID. We've put out a pickup on Hack, with mug shots and all, but nothing's shown so far."

"Could the body be Sigmund's?" I asked.

"We tried to check that out. Even had Wayne Cutter take a look at the body. He admitted he'd hardly seen the boy since he went to college, but he looked at the hands close and finally said no, it didn't seem likely. The hands were too old, and the fingernails too dirty. He claimed Sig kept them real neat and trim. Then all of a sudden he switched lines, said maybe he'd got careless in college. I got the sneaky notion he wanted me to think he knew it was his son, but couldn't quite handle the idea and was trying to kid himself."

"You mean he figures the boy killed Hack and is trying to make you think there's no use looking for him?"

"Yeah. When I asked how about we bring his mother around for a look, he got madder'n hell. Asked what kind of a sadistic moron would ask a mother to look at her murdered son."

"Could you get fingerprints of Sigmund from anything in his home, maybe letters to the family?"

"I checked that too. Like I say, he hasn't been living at home for nearly four years, and so far nobody we've found admits to having letters around from him in the last year. It's hard to believe he's not been in touch at all, and if he did write, that they wouldn't have hung on to the letters."

I looked at Mary Jo. She shook her head.

"He's never written to me. We have seen each other almost every day since he started school, so there was no occasion. I don't believe there'd even be any prints in the room he used. It's been cleaned thoroughly since he left about two weeks ago."

Ahern asked for her okay to have the Pine Island cops check her place, at least give it a try. She agreed, even talking with the police there when Ahern made the call.

I told Mary Jo she was doing the right thing. She sighed. "I hope to God you're right," she said.

28

"HAVE YOU TALKED with the younger brother?" I asked Ahern.

He shook his head. "His mother claims he's visiting family in New York State. Camping somewhere, so he's out of reach. I told her to run him down or we'd see the cops did it. She said I'd hear."

Mary Jo looked at me. "Let's go talk with Doreen."

Ahern liked that idea and suggested we let him know how it went.

Giselle answered the door. She looked tired, but her hair was neatly brushed, her red lipstick glowed, and she was wearing a blue dress that matched her eyes. She took in Mary Jo with something shy of approval.

I introduced them and said we wanted to talk with her mother. Giselle nodded, led us into the living room, and went upstairs after her mother.

"Now why do you suppose she gave me the icy eye?" Mary Jo asked softly. "Are you two well acquainted?"

"Not that well."

"I'd swear this was a jealous woman. Isn't she a little young for you?"

"Her problem's got nothing to do with me. She's probably suspicious that you were too cozy with her brother in Minneapolis."

"Ah." She got up and wandered the room, taking in the furnishings and bric-a-brac. She hadn't made it half way around when Giselle returned.

"I'm sorry," she said to me, "Mother doesn't care to see you right now, but she'd like to ask Mary Jo some questions if she's willing to come up to her room for a few minutes."

Mary Jo got to her feet and followed her toward the stairs without glancing my way.

I tried my own tour of the room and got hung up at the bookshelf, full of heavy stuff like *The Decline and Fall of the Roman Empire*, Macaulay's *History of England*, and complete sets of Jane Austen's and George Eliot's novels. The one surprise was a copy of Dorothy Parker's *Enough Rope*. I sat down and read it, looking for the short, familiar poems. Mary Jo returned as I was reading "Neither Bloody nor Bowed": "They say of me, and so they should/It's doubtful if I come to good." It sounded like the story of my life.

Mary Jo's expression told me she didn't want to talk here. We left the house without a word and went out to my Model T. She didn't speak until we had traveled about four blocks.

"Well?" I said.

She shook her head. "At times it was almost as if this were a different person from the woman I talked with last night on the telephone. The cold calm was gone—she was intense, and almost emotional. The first thing she asked was, when did I see Sigmund last, and how was he acting? She seemed upset that he left my place. Even acted at first as if I might be lying. Then she suddenly changed direction— asked when you and I met, and what I thought of you. I told her. We agreed that you were hard to figure, not at all as simple as you let on. Then she went into this theory that Sigmund suspects she and Wayne would do anything to keep Lilybell from snooping into the family history because she might uncover scandals about Colonel Cutter's actions during the Civil War. She suspects, she said, that Gunnar telephoned Sigmund to tell him his suspicions, and that Sigmund then dashed off to try and warn Lilybell, maybe even protect her, since he's hopelessly romantic."

"Where'd he get such an idea? Was she maybe talking with Uriah Hack when Gunnar listened in?" I asked.

"She certainly didn't tell me that."

"So now she's in a sweat because she doesn't know where the boys are?"

"Yes."

"Do you know if the cops asked Wayne to identify the body of the guy who had Uriah's wallet?"

She nodded.

"Wayne assured them that with the face blown away, he had no idea who it could be. And he told Doreen it was too old to be Sigmund."

"Did she believe him?"

"Well, she tried to give me the idea she wasn't totally reassured. I can't put my finger on why I think she doesn't believe Wayne really cares about Sigmund, but it's a feeling I've got. Somehow talking with her always makes me feel I'm being led with great deliberation along paths of her choosing."

"What else?"

"She asked me if I thought you would try and find Sigmund for her. She's willing to pay for it, with the understanding that if you do find him, you don't inform the police."

"If she wants me for that, why doesn't she ask me direct?"

She smiled. "I'm not certain. Probably she wanted to see how I'd react, thinking it might clue her into how you would.

I'm trying to tell you, she's a very calculating, manipulative woman. She might even have hoped I'd try to talk you into taking the job."

"I just find him, report back, and she writes a check. Is that it?"

She nodded.

"What if he's dead?"

She made a face and shook her head.

"What'd she offer you to do the coaxing?"

That got me a mildly withering look. "Who's been coaxing?"

"Nobody. Not directly, anyway."

She grinned again. "Actually she hinted it would pay me to get you interested. I didn't ask how much."

"Did she ask if we'd been making out?"

"Come on, Carl, she's not the sort of woman who'd ask a question like that. She just assumes you're interested and that it might be easier for me to influence you."

"Okay, where's she think her boy is?"

"She wants to believe he's back at my place in his room. I don't think she has any idea where else he might be. If she did, she wouldn't be trying to get you on his trail."

"Has she heard from Hack?"

"She didn't say, and I didn't ask. It's not likely she'd admit any connection."

"What about her story to Ahern that the brothers are somewhere East, camping?"

"She didn't mention it. I suspect that was a stall—though it's possible Gunnar's there."

I asked if there was anyone around her place in Minneapolis who'd check and see if Sigmund had come back. She said yes, there was a maintenance man who would look for her.

He did, and the answer was no. The house was as she had left it.

29

WE STOPPED FOR coffee at a small café on Phillips Avenue, and Mary Jo asked about my earlier interview with Wayne. I told it as remembered, and she nodded wisely.

"I think it might be a good idea for me to talk with him alone. You two are so totally different, he can't begin to understand anything about you or your thinking. My closeness to Sigmund the last four years might make him loosen up if I handle it right. Anyway, it's worth a try. While I'm working on him, why don't you call on Doreen again? Or maybe it'd be better if you work on the daughter. I think she's definitely interested in you, and she's bound to be worried about Sigmund, and probably Gunnar too. From things Sigmund's told me, I believe they've been very close in the past. She's bound to be worried about the boys, and if handled right, she could be helpful. It's pretty clear the boys were alienated from both parents—maybe she is too."

I agreed to give it a whirl. Giselle answered the telephone on the first ring.

"Expecting a call?" I asked.

"I was hoping to hear from Sigmund."

"Would you take a walk with me if I came around?"

"What for?"

"I think you know."

There was a moment of silence. Then she agreed.

She was on the porch when I arrived and met me on the walk, looking freshly made-up and wearing a red dress with white ruffles. We strolled along a walk shaded by tall dark elms with browning leaves.

"How's your mother doing?" I asked.

She tilted her head as she looked my way. "Remember I told you she wouldn't look upset if she woke and found her bed on fire?"

"Yeah."

"That's all changed. Now she's worried. Dad stays away from the house. She makes telephone calls when she thinks I'm far enough away not to overhear. You know the saddest thing? Everybody in the family comes to her with their troubles, but there's no one she can turn to for help. She can't admit she needs any. It's like she's convinced that if anyone thought she had any vulnerability, they'd lose faith in her. She's simply got to be above us all. Isn't that sad?"

"You know why she told Ahern that Sigmund was with his brother out East?"

"She doesn't want the police to find him. I'm not sure why that frightens her, but it's possible she thinks he might do something foolish. He's terribly independent, and she thinks he might offend any police who tried to pick him up or even question him."

"How'd he feel about Wilda Mahon?"

Her eyebrows lifted. "He respected her. We all did. Why do you ask? He certainly wouldn't go to her to hide. In a town that small he'd be conspicuous as a giraffe on the prairie."

"Were they close?"

"I suppose so, in a way. She was always good to us, very patient but firm. She never pretended to be a mother."

"Where do you think Sigmund is?"

"I'm afraid to think about it. I can't imagine he's simply off somewhere hiding. It's not in his nature. I think something absolutely horrid has happened—we all do—and none of us is able to deal with it. We're all afraid we might be to blame in some way."

"You think your dad hired Hack to kill Lilybell?"

"He wouldn't hire him right out, no. He might have gotten in touch, passed the word that Lilybell was bad-mouthing the colonel. He knew Uriah wasn't exactly stable, if you know what I mean."

"You mean he was a maniac."

"I'm afraid so."

"Yeah, but so far, if he's alive, too smart for any of us."

"That's not believable either. None of this is. I'm going home, I don't want to think or talk about it anymore."

When we got to her front porch steps, she turned and faced me.

"Maybe it would be better if you just went back home and forgot about all of this, and us. Nothing good will come of it all. Nothing."

"It doesn't seem likely," I admitted, "but it's not something I can just walk away from. I'll be in touch."

She glanced back at the house, then moved my way, took my arm, and started us walking again.

"There's a way I might be able to reach Gunnar," she said, not looking at me. "If I can manage that, and get him to talk with you, will you keep it quiet? I mean, not tell the police? Maybe you can talk him into telling where Sigmund might be. Make him understand how terrified we—no, make it me—how terrified I am about his safety. And that it's im-

portant we find out what he's doing and how dangerous it is
if Uriah is still alive, and hunting for him. Will you promise
me you'll not tell if he calls you?"

"Damn right."

She said if she reached him she'd ask him to call me at
my hotel in the evening, and we left it at that.

30

THE CALL CAME just before ten that night. I had given the hotel's public phone number to Giselle. I was waiting in the lobby and picked up the receiver before the end of the first ring.

"My sister says you're not big, but you whipped Tiny Fox. Is that really so?"

"It's pretty close. Why's that important?"

"I don't know. You been a cop too, she says."

"I've been a lot of things, Gunnar. Where are you?"

"She told me I shouldn't say. I can tell you I'm not out East and I'm scared about Sigmund."

"Then he's not with you?"

"I haven't seen him since he left for Corden."

"What was his plan?"

"He was going to see Lilybell."

"Why?"

"Well, from what I heard, he thought she might be in trouble, and he wanted to help. Sigmund's kind of big on being a hero."

"How come you're hiding out?"

"Sig told me to."

"Why?"

"Because Hack knew we were on Lilybell's side."

"How'd Sig know what she was up to?"

"I overheard Dad talking with Uriah Hack on the telephone about her. He was telling him that Lilybell had killed her husband and gotten away with it and now she was slandering our family, the colonel specially. He said she was in Corden trying to dig up dirt and make trouble because she hated all the Cutters and Foxes and would do anything to hurt them. He said somebody had to get to her and stop all of that."

"So you called Sig and told him what you'd heard?"

"Well, sure. I knew how he'd feel about it."

"How'd Sig get to Corden?"

"Hitchhiked. He always traveled like that."

I thought for a few seconds. "Look, let's face the facts and level, okay?"

"I don't think we know any facts."

"We know Sig went to Corden. We know Lilybell was murdered there and that this guy, Uriah Hack, was in the hotel. If Hack killed her and Sig caught him in the act, somebody else got killed. Sig didn't have a car—"

"He could've taken Hack's."

"Yeah, if he killed him first. Was he armed?"

"He never had a gun I know of."

"If he was going to arm himself, what'd you figure he'd take, a knife, a club of some kind?"

"I don't know. That's not anything we ever got into. He's a good wrestler, did some fencing at the U. But he sure didn't carry around his foil. If he was mad enough, I'd guess he'd just go hand to hand."

"Against a man with an ice pick?"

"He might. He's awful fast."

THE ICE PICK ARTIST / 155

"Who's his best friend?"

"Me."

"Outside of family."

There'd been a good high school buddy, but in his senior year his family moved to California, and that ended it. The guy wasn't a letter writer.

"How long did Sig tell you to hide?"

He was silent for a couple seconds, then said, " 'Til he called me."

"So why hasn't he called?"

"Because things aren't settled yet."

"Why wouldn't he call just to reassure you?"

"He's probably got other worries."

"The only one that'd keep him from calling you was if he'd killed Hack and was afraid telling you about it would make you an accomplice. Isn't that right?"

"I don't know."

"Come on, Gunnar, get real. There are only two things that could've happened. Your brother killed Hack, or Hack killed him. If your brother did the killing, the sooner we find him and get the facts, the better our chances will be to prove it was self-defense. If Hack killed your brother, we've got to find the son of a bitch and see he gets his."

"They say he's already dead."

"We don't know that. The cops think the body might have been somebody's else's, planted to make it look like Hack, so everybody'd quit looking for him."

"They think the body's Sig?" He almost choked on that.

"Probably not."

"Thank God."

"So come home and ease things for your folks."

"I'd probably make things worse. My story'll make the cops think Dad had something to do with it all."

"You think he did?"

"Well, don't you?"

"It's possible. That doesn't mean he hired Hack, but he might've egged him on, since they say Hack was ready to believe Lilybell had killed his old buddy Felix."

I asked about girls, and Gunnar said there'd been one that was pretty close, Marlene Drew. Her father was in politics and had a lot of money.

He gave me Marlene's father's name and promised to call back tomorrow at about the same time if he thought of anything new. Before he hung up, I asked if he could explain why his brother, if he were all right, wouldn't have been in touch. He hemmed and hawed around awhile, but finally admitted that I was probably right, he'd probably feel any contact with the family might make them vulnerable as accessories. Being the kind of guy he was, he simply wouldn't risk that.

The next morning I called Minneapolis information, got the Drew number, and reached Marlene's mother, who informed me her daughter was unavailable and asked what was the business of my call.

I explained that Sigmund was missing and we needed his help in checking out a murder in Corden.

She informed me, in icily polite terms, that the Cutter family had already been in touch with Marlene regarding their son's whereabouts and had been informed they knew nothing helpful. She referred me to Wayne Cutter.

31

MARY JO TOLD me that Wayne Cutter had been polite, even cordial, but not helpful. He denied having any notion of where his son might be hiding out, and insisted he'd had no contact with Uriah Hack, direct or otherwise. When she asked if Sigmund hadn't had a girlfriend at school, Wayne said yes, he had—he'd called her parents' home, and the mother told him their daughter was visiting friends in England. She added that Marlene had not been seeing Sigmund for some time before she left.

"I got the feeling." Mary Jo told me, "that they were implying she had been unhappy with him and made the trip to England to break up their relationship."

A call to Murduff at his gas station got me his young attendant, who said the boss had taken a trip and wasn't expected back for a day or two. He thought he might've gone to Aberdeen.

In the morning I called his house, and after several rings his wife answered. She wasn't any friendlier than when I'd called before, and told me abruptly her husband was gone, and good riddance. She didn't know where, didn't care, and wasn't going to talk about it. Then she told me he was a selfish, unreliable, philandering rat and expanded on the subject. Eventually I bulldozed a couple questions into the tirade. He had left, supposedly on a business trip, the day after my call, she said, and she'd heard nothing since.

"Has he taken off like this before?"

She said yes, but admitted it had never been for more than one night other times. No, he hadn't told her anything, except that he would be back with a bundle of money. I asked if her husband had ever mentioned a man named Uriah Hack, and after some rambling she admitted the name sounded familiar. I strongly suspected she had not been in the habit of recording her husband's reports on his world.

"Does you son live at home?" I asked.

"No. Too smart to hang around here. Went to St. Paul."

She wasn't clear about how he made his living. He didn't write or telephone except to ask for money, but, she hastened to assure me, that wasn't often.

I called Sergeant Ahern, told him about Murduff's taking off, and explained that he was about the same age, height, and weight as Hack. "Maybe he thought he could pick up some hush money and Hack planted him, figuring his carcass would throw us off."

"I don't picture Hack using a shotgun," he said.

"Maybe he didn't, originally. More than likely he used his ice pick first, then blew the face away so he couldn't be identified."

"Okay, I'll check out the coroner, see if he can take another look. Since this isn't settled yet, I think the stiff is still in cold storage."

The next day Giselle called me. Her brother Gunnar had heard from Marlene, who claimed that Sigmund hadn't been in touch for well over a week.

"According to your father, Marlene's in England. She call from there?"

"No. She's here in Sioux Falls."

"How come?"

"She says she came hoping to find Sigmund. We've talked a lot, and she wants to meet you."

"Where?"

"On the Big Sioux River by the waterfall. She's a little strange, Carl. She doesn't want me or anybody else along. I'm not even sure what she has in mind—she's very secretive."

I asked when we were to meet and what she looked like.

"This afternoon. At three. She's quite small and slender, with reddish hair, a thin nose, high cheekbones, and a broad forehead. She's one of those people that practically look through you, and her dress is too short and usually red."

"You don't like her much?"

"That's not it—but she sort of puts other women off. You'll probably go for her big. She likes to make men feel important. She said she'd be waiting for you by the big rocks at the foot of the Sioux waterfall."

The dress wasn't very short, but the rest of the description fit like a new girdle.

She looked me over as I approached and frowned. It gave me the feeling she figured I was no more than what she had expected, but less than she had hoped for. She also looked behind me and around, as though expecting to find someone tailing me.

It was pretty plain I wasn't the kind of guy she would try to make feel important.

"If you have any imagination at all," she said as we sat down on boulders, facing each other, "you can imagine how desperate I must be to ask for a meeting with someone like you. I've decided to try it because there aren't any other choices—I've no confidence in the local police—but frankly,

I think it's idiotic to try and solve this riddle with help from a renegade like you. It only seems worth a shot because you sound unconventional enough to maybe understand Sigmund. He has a strange, childish faith in his grandfather, and an almost pathological hatred of his father."

"When you say his grandfather, you mean the colonel, right?"

Her eyebrows elevated. "So you dug that up? All right, maybe you're smarter than you look. In that case you can probably imagine the bind he was in, compelled to defend a woman who wanted to expose his beloved grandpa as a villain. Sigmund went to Corden to see Lilybell not only to warn her against the danger of her trying to dig up dirt on his grandpa but to try and convince her that Colonel Cutter was really a great man. Somehow, Sigmund always felt he could persuade anyone to his way of thinking, except Wayne. Gunnar and Giselle both want to believe you understand this, and that you're more interested in getting at the truth of what happened than in just finding a fall guy—which is what they think the police are after."

"Where do you think Sigmund is?"

She stared across the water, frowning. It gave her a tragic expression and showed her fine profile. After a moment she looked at me directly again.

"I think what you said to Gunnar was probably right. Sigmund fought with that man, Hack, and killed him, and has run away. Maybe to California or even East. Like you said, he wouldn't want the family to be hurt, trying to protect or hide him."

"Or you, either."

She looked tragic some more. "That's right."

"Why'd you want to talk to me?"

"Well, I thought, since you've been working so close with the police, that maybe you knew something I didn't. I'm really

in love with Sigmund, you know, and I can't help being terrified that just maybe something happened to him, that maybe
he was even killed."

"Okay, let me run something by you. Say Sig showed up
right after Hack killed Lilybell, tapped on her door, and getting no answer, pushed in. Hack was behind the door and
coldcocked him, carried him down to his car, and later got in
touch with his father. He might even have demanded money
to deliver the boy alive. You think from what Sigmund's told
you of his old man that Wayne would pay to keep him from
being killed?"

"No. From everything Sigmund's told me, his father's so
cold-blooded he'd never give it a thought."

"But you don't think what I've said happened."

"Haven't you talked with Doreen?"

"No. You think I should try?"

"I'd think you would. You know her at all?"

"Only what I've heard from Sigmund and Giselle. He
thinks she goes along with anything his father decides.
Giselle and I aren't convinced of that."

"You know his sister?"

"We've talked on the phone several times. I like her."

She gave me a stern look. "She trusts you. I hope that's
not a mistake."

"So do I."

I asked where she was staying, and she said with a friend on
the north side. She gave me a telephone number where I could
reach her, but claimed she didn't remember the address.

When I went back to the hotel for dinner, the desk clerk
told me I'd had a call from a Sergeant Ahern. He wanted me
to call him back.

"Carl," he said, the moment I spoke, "a body's shown up
in the Tanner Hotel, on the edge of town. It fits your description of Uriah Hack right down to dirty fingernails."

32

THE HOTEL MANAGER reported that his chamber-maid had found the body on the floor of the room. The damage had been done with something like an ice pick, the coroner thought. Ahern had learned that a doctor had been called to that same room to treat a young man suffering a severe con-cussion, supposedly from a fall out of a car, reported by the man who had taken the room and called himself Bob Jones. He had claimed the young man was his son. When the body was discovered by the chambermaid, the local law figured this must be the suspect in the Corden killing.

"Think you can make a positive ID?" I asked.

"Yeah. He had a record of assault in Minneapolis. We'll check his prints out."

"Has this got you thinking what I'm thinking?"

"That Sigmund's alive?"

"Yeah."

"It figures. I'm going around to the Cutters'. Want to come along?"

"I'll be right over."

We went in Ahern's car. He told me he'd talked with Doreen on the telephone and told her that there had been a new development in the case. He glanced at me and frowned. "I'm gonna be a real bastard. Tell her we found another body. Ask if she's willing to try and identify it."

Giselle answered the door and led us into the living room, where Doreen sat knitting something bright green.

"Another body's been found," Ahern told her. "Now I hate to do this, but I'd like to ask you to come downtown and see if you can identify it."

She met his eyes directly.

"You think it's Sigmund."

"No. But we want to be sure."

She looked at me. "Whose idea was this?"

"It was mine," said Ahern.

"I see." She set her knitting down on the floor next to the chair. "Why aren't you asking my husband this time?"

"He didn't appreciate my asking him the last time. I got the feeling this whole business is more important to you than to him."

"What you really think is I'm more vulnerable, isn't that it? All right. I'll come along."

Giselle wanted to come too, but her mother told her she should stay home.

Doreen didn't speak on the drive downtown or when we went into the room where the body lay covered on a table. Ahern pulled the cover off the head and Doreen's face stiffened, but her eyes were steady.

"Know him?"

"That's Uriah Hack," she said.

"So you knew him?"

She turned her face and looked at me.

"I saw him once or twice, years ago, at family gatherings. I paid attention to his face because he was already something of a family disgrace. I haven't seen him for years, never even talked with him. It was a face you don't forget. I felt sorry for him."

"Why?"

"He made me think of Gustave Doré's illustrations of the damned in Dante's *Inferno*. It seemed prophetic."

Ahern looked at me, and back at her.

"How well did your husband know Hack?"

"What are you getting at?"

"Quite a bit. You want to go where we can sit down and talk?"

We went into an adjacent office, where a clerk go up from a typewriter desk when Ahern told her we needed the room for a few minutes. I took the abandoned chair, Doreen sat in the armchair, and Ahern stayed on his feet.

"I'm going to run what we know by you, and I'd like any help we can get, because we got an—excuse me—hell of a job here sorting things out. Everything uncovered so far tells us Hack went to Corden to kill Lilybell Fox, and did it. We also got good reasons to believe your son was at the hotel that night. The description of him given by Mrs. Wilcox is one people recognize—just like I think you did when you heard it the first time. Now we know Hack was murdered. Nobody knows, or will tell us, where Sigmund is, but we know he was mad at your husband, and we have good reason to believe he was tipped off about Hack's assignment in Corden. We think he went to warn Mrs. Fox. Carl here thinks he might have tried to convince her that old Colonel Cutter wasn't a bad guy, like she'd been trying to prove. We know he was at the movie theater that night—there're witnesses to that. It could be Mrs. Fox was dead by the time he got back to the hotel and tried to contact her. We can only guess that he followed Hack somehow, or had some notion where he'd be heading, and went after him. Everything we've heard about Sigmund makes it seem likely he was mad as hell about the murder and tried to avenge it—"

"That," interrupted Doreen, "is pure poppycock. I won't deny he's impulsive and righteous-minded enough to have attacked Uriah if he caught him at the scene. I wouldn't dispute that for a moment. But he would absolutely not run him down after the murder to avenge Lilybell. He didn't know her personally. Sigmund is all impulse and spontaneousness. He hasn't the patience for deliberate pursuit."

"Doesn't take much after his father, eh?"

Her red lips tightened. "What's that supposed to imply?"

"Lilybell's snooping would damage your husband more than anybody else. We all know Wayne's been thinking of running for governor, or maybe senator. He wouldn't have been exactly tickled pink with reports on what a pirate his old man was, or that Wayne's's real father was the colonel, not brother Vic, who probably croaked with a little help from his wife."

"Victor didn't need any help from Mattie to die. He got it all from a bottle."

"Okay, we're not gonna worry about ancient history. But something you got to face, Mrs. Cutter, is the fact that your husband set up things so it looks like the murderer is your son. And the way things stand, we got nobody else to put it on. Now maybe the way things have gone, you're sore at your son too, but I don't believe you're ready to let him pay the whole load on this mess There's another thing you should know. We got a witness who says your younger son, Gunnar, overheard you talking to somebody about how Lilybell was bad-mouthing the colonel and Wayne wanted her to shut up. Do you know for a fact that your husband put Hack up to killing Lilybell Fox?"

Doreen stared at him for a moment, then carefully got up, tucked her purse under her elbow, and started for the door.

When she had her hand on the knob she turned, frowning.

"I believe," she said, "that a wife can't testify against her husband. I'll be talking with our lawyer about that, and other things. Good day."

"There's something else you ought to know, Mrs. Cutter. Yesterday Hack brought the local doctor up to his hotel room to treat a young man for brain concussion. The description of the young man fits Sigmund. There was no sign of Sigmund around, and Hack's car was gone."

For a few seconds Doreen stared at Ahern, then she nodded and walked out.

When the door had closed quietly behind her, Ahern sighed, walked over, and sat down in the chair she had abandoned.

"Well, I blew it."

"I don't think so," I said. "I think our friend Wayne Cutter is in deep dung."

"How do you figure?"

"I don't think she and her hubby are together on this thing. If it comes down to whose hide gets stretched on the wall, she'll make it be Wayne, not her son. What she's going to do is figure what she can work out for Sigmund. Make him a hero, a savior."

"That'd be a good trick."

"A good lawyer could do it. And Doreen can afford the best around. The key is getting Sigmund to help his own case—prove he was positive his father was behind Lilybell's murder, and that he, Sigmund, flipped when he found Lilybell murdered. You've got to remember, Wayne Cutter's not the colonel. From everything I've heard about the old man, he was an artist at turning people into puppets and spreading the old oil. Nothing I've heard about Wayne tells me he picked up any of that talent, and I'd guess a smart lawyer could carve him up on the witness stand."

Ahern leaned forward, resting his elbows on the desk. "There's another little hitch in all this. Murduff. If Sigmund killed him, you kind of shoot the whole business of the boy being a hero."

"Maybe," I admitted. "The one thing that makes me think it isn't likely our boy did the Murduff thing is that there'd be no real good reason for him to try and make it look like Murduff was Hack. There's no percentage. I've got a wild notion what might have happened, but we can't make anything of it until we find Sigmund."

"You got any ideas how we're going to manage that?"

"Yeah. Put a tail on the girlfriend, Marlene Drew."

All I could offer was the telephone number she'd given me. With that, Ahern said there'd be no trouble getting the address. His sister-in-law worked for the telephone company.

33

T H A T   N I G H T   I got a telephone call from an attorney
named Fitzsimmons. He said he thought we might have interests in common, and would I care to meet with him? I said,
sure, if it wouldn't cost me anything.

He chuckled. "A little time, is all. Know where
Thompson's Café is?"

I didn't, but he told me, and half an hour later we were
sitting across from each other in a corner booth near the
kitchen entrance to the dining room.

He was a stocky Irishman, with curly hair thinning at the
top and graying around the temples. The blue eyes behind
rimless glasses looked innocent except when he asked questions. Then they took on an illegal sharpness.

"I'll level with you all the way," he said. "I've talked with
the Cutters and Marlene Drew, and they have a feeling that
your interest in this Lilybell Fox killing, and what followed,
comes from your sympathy for her and a certain open-mind-
edness about the—what shall I call them—emotional reac-

tions of those who knew her and were involved in all of the ramifications of her death."

I drank some coffee and watched him.

"You have no official police connection?" he asked.

"You got it."

"But you are on good terms with the principal investigator, Sergeant Ahern, right?"

"So far."

He grinned, all Irish. "Well, don't worry—I'm not about to ask you to betray any trust or reveal any strategies. I'm talking to you, frankly, because the Cutters and Miss Drew all seem to feel you're sympathetic toward Sigmund, whatever happened, and that it might help if I could get your thoughts on the defense we will develop. I know you've had previous experience with murder investigations, and impressive success in working out details. Would you be willing to tell me what you think happened in this case?"

"No. If you're taking the case, you must have a pretty clear story to work from. You tell me what it is, I'll tell you how it fits with the evidence I know about so far, and we can take it from there. What's Sigmund's story?"

He pulled out a package of Luckies, offered me one, and lit us both up with his silver lighter.

"All right. As I understand it, Sigmund learned from his brother that Lilybell was in Corden seeking information about Colonel Cutter, and that Uriah Hack, a notorious killer, had been convinced by Wayne Cutter that she was responsible for the death of her husband, a close friend of Hack's, and that Hack was going there to kill her. Sigmund hitchhiked to Corden, spent the early evening at the local cinema, went to the hotel, learned where her room was, and at approximately eleven-thirty went up and knocked on her door. When there was no response, he pushed inside. Hack stepped from behind the door and struck him on the back of the head with a blackjack, knocking him unconscious.

"From the damage to his skull, it's obvious Hack hit him several times, causing a severe concussion. Sigmund eventually came to in a dark room on a cot. His head ached horribly, and his legs and hands were bound. He heard talking in the next room and then a strangled cry, and a gunshot. He said it sounded loud enough to be a cannon. When the room's door opened a moment later, he pretended he was still unconscious. Then the door closed.

He lost consciousness until later, when he felt himself being dragged off the cot, lifted, and carried outside. It was night. His head ached so intensely he couldn't think of anything else. He wanted to ask for water but was afraid it would only bring another assault. The next time he became conscious he realized he had been untied and was on a bed. His head was bandaged. Very carefully he sat up and, after a brief fit of dizziness, got to his feet. He guessed he was in a hotel room, since there was a washbasin with a large white ceramic water pitcher on the bureau near the bed. He heard footsteps in the hall, moved to the bureau, got the pitcher, and stepped behind the door. When a man came in, he hit him on the back of the head with the pitcher. Sigmund says he went down like a felled ox, but then began to roll over. Sigmund saw an ice pick strapped to his leg, just above the ankle. He snatched it free and stabbed the man until he became still."

Fitzsimmons's blue eyes stared at me a moment, probing for a reaction.

I nodded, hoping it looked encouraging.

"You have to remember, he was in pain, he was very afraid, but he was also positive this was the man who had murdered Lilybell, and who obviously knew Sigmund was the only witness against him. He was quite positive he had to kill him or die."

I nodded again.

The lawyer didn't quite smile.

"Sigmund rested several minutes, trying to get over his dizziness and exhaustion, then checked the hall and found it deserted. He went downstairs and out a doorway at the foot of the steps. It was night. The street was unknown to him, and deserted. He located Hack's car, identifying it from what he'd seen while in the backseat, went back upstairs, took the keys from Hack's pocket, returned to the car, and fled in it."

"Where is he now?"

"I don't know." He smiled at my expression. "Honestly. He's being taken care of and doesn't want to be disturbed until he's more himself. He's had a traumatic experience and is not in any condition to face cross-examination and all of that."

"Okay, let me get something else straight. Are you working for the Cutter family, or just Doreen—or maybe Sigmund?"

"Mrs. Cutter has consulted me. I've not talked with her husband."

"So in this case the wife can say all she wants about the husband as long as she's not doing it in court under oath."

"You have a fine grasp of the basic facts."

"And one of these facts is, the lady intends to put the screws to hubby, isn't that it?"

"She wants to place the responsibility for what has happened directly where it belongs. She believes that her husband deliberately goaded Uriah Hack into an attack on Lilybell Fox and is therefore at the very least an accessory to murder. She believes that he was responsible for the subsequent attack on her son and equally responsible for the killing, in self-defense, of Hack by Sigmund. She believes her husband should be brought to account for his actions and accept responsibility for all that came of this miserable business."

"Is she suing for divorce?"

"In due time."

"So what do you really want from me?"

He looked up, sighted the waitress, and gestured toward his coffee cup. She delivered, freshened us both, and moved off.

He put sugar and cream in his cup, stirred it gently, took a sip, and sat back.

"Sigmund wants to talk with you. But first he wants your word that you will not tell the police where he is until after your conference with him."

"Okay. Where do I go?"

34

"IT'S MY UNCLE Percy's farm," Marlene told me as we headed west of Sioux Falls. "He's a bachelor. Doesn't work his land anymore, just lives in the back room downstairs. Daddy supports him. He's very old and is taken care of by Aunt Myrtle, who's never been married either. Percy's my favorite relative. He thinks I'm great."

"Did he know Sigmund before he moved in?"

"No. I asked if he could come, and he said if he was my friend he was welcome. They get along fine."

I parked near the side door, which admitted us to a dinky vestibule with stairs on the right going to the dugout basement, and two steps up to the kitchen straight ahead. It smelled of fresh-baked bread with a hint of soap. Aunt Myrtle was a stocky woman with thick ankles, barely revealed by her long black-and-white checked skirt. Her mixed gray and dark brown hair was fixed in tight waves that framed her wrinkled face. Her pale blue eyes took me in through thick-lensed bifocals, and she smiled with her thin mouth closed. She acknowledged our introduction by Marlene with a bob of her head, and we moved through a small dining room into the parlor beyond.

The room was quite dark. All the shades were drawn to the sill and stirred occasionally as the late-afternoon breeze came through the open windows beyond.

Sigmund sat in an easy chair, his feet resting on a small stool. The head bandage and his pale face made him look like a turbaned ghost. His teeth gleamed as he took me in, grinning.

"Well," he said, "the rustic Sherlock Holmes, I presume."

"Don't be like that," Marlene scolded. "You want him to think you've had brain damage?"

"I wouldn't swear I haven't," he said, still watching me. "Take a chair. I'm glad to see you. Everyone's been so worried about keeping me undercover, I'm beginning to feel like a hermit. What's the story out there? Does everybody think I'm a mass murderer?"

"I haven't taken a poll, but mostly everybody's confused, like me."

I sat, rolled and lit a cigarette, and asked if he had any idea where he was the night he heard the shotgun fired.

"Not the foggiest. I just know it wasn't where I came to the second time in the hotel. The first place wasn't a bedroom, more like a big closet where they keep linens. There were shelves and just this cot I was on. No windows. The one door."

"You hear anything before the shotgun blast?"

"I think there was something like a gasp, then a grunt, or groan. Nothing's really clear through that time. My head hurt so bad I wanted to yell, but I thought if I did, my skull would shatter."

"Did the name Murdoff, on the hotel register in Corden, mean anything to you?"

"Well, yeah. I knew there was this cousin from Aberdeen

with a name close to that. It didn't occur to me that Hack would
use it, so I was really mixed up. But then I decided maybe they
were in cahoots. What gets me worst is that I thought I was being
so clever, you know? Figured if I got in to see Lilybell before
midnight, she'd be okay. That the murderer wouldn't strike 'til
after midnight. I went to the movie to kill time."

"What'd you see when you went in Lilybell's room?"

"Damn little—except that her arm was hanging over the
edge of the bed. Before that really registered, I got hit. I
remember my knee seemed to crack as I fell, then my head
caught it again, and that was all. Until I came to in the linen
room, or whatever it was."

I took him over everything he could remember after the
blackjacking, and the story he told was a carbon copy of what
I'd heard from his lawyer. He only added that he had chosen
to get help from Marlene because she was imaginative and
smart enough to make him think she'd be more help than
anyone else he could turn to, and besides, he was in love with
her.

I had the feeling he got the love line in just on time to
keep from getting another knot on his head, Marlene was
glowering at him, and the magic word hadn't come early
enough to suit her.

"What made you think you could attack Hack when you
did?" I asked.

"Plain and simple panic. Here's this guy that's already
nearly brained me, and he's got this ugly mug, and there's
nothing in his eyes but murder—I just knew I had to do
something now. And I don't know, he seemed kind of distracted. I was able to convince myself he figured I was a total
basket case and could be surprised. I came to when he was
out, got up, moved around a little, looking for something I
could hit him with. There just wasn't anything there but the
water pitcher, and I hefted it, found it was really heavy and

solid, but still something I could swing. When I heard sounds in the hall, I pulled his stunt and waited behind the door. He had his head down a little—I doubt he even saw I wasn't on the bed before I hit him. Then he was on the floor, sort of scrabbling around, with his pants cuffs up. I saw the ice pick and grabbed for it because the pitcher broke when I belted him. He was getting to his knees, and there just wasn't any choice. I caught him in the forearm first, then the shoulder, and just kept going at him until he was stretched out."

The exertion and panic made him faint for a time, but he managed to go through Hack's pockets and come up with car and room keys. When he went through the lobby downstairs he saw the wall clock, which told him it was 1:30 A.M. He went out to look for the car—not a lot of trouble, because there were only three at the curb out front. The key he had fit the second one he tried.

"Let's go back to when you first woke up untied. Didn't Hack ever try to talk to you?"

"Not while I was conscious."

"I got a little problem with your story, Sigmund. You wake up in this room, you've been untied, and somebody's repaired your head. You get up and find out you can move okay, and you get this pitcher and wait behind the door when you hear a sound in the hall. How'd you know it was the guy that hit you? When did you ever see his face?"

"Never. You're right. I could've brained some doctor, or somebody who'd found me in a ditch and brought me in. But I'm trying to tell you, I wasn't exactly thinking straight, you know? Somebody nearly brained me. I'd been moved around, handled like a sack of flour. The only thing in my head beyond pain was survival—and yeah, I wanted back at the son of a bitch who'd flattened me. And the minute I could see his face, after belting him with the pitcher, I knew who he was. That's a kisser you don't forget from any angle."

35

I HEADED BACK toward town alone, intending to see Ahern and tell him what I'd learned, but finally decided to try another shot at the old monster, Tiny Fox.

Tiny was sitting at a cluttered desk, scowling at a file between big paws, as I came in. He showed no surprise at the sight of me.

"Your forgot your cop friend," he said.

"I figured maybe we could level better without him around."

He leaned back in the swivel chair, which creaked under the load, and nodded toward the chair in front of his desk. I parked, crossed my legs, and offered my old-buddy grin.

"Your want to tell me about Hack's call to you just after he coldcocked the Cutter kid?"

His dog eyes didn't so much as blink.

"Now where'd you get a notion like that?" he asked.

"Been talking with Sigmund. His story is fishier than dead carp on a beach. But it got me thinking about you."

"Yeah?"

"I figure when Hack dropped Sigmund in Lilybell's room, right after he'd murdered the woman, he was a little more than surprised to recognize the night visitor as Wayne Cutter's kid. Now I never figured Hack was the brightest bird I've met, but even he had to wonder how come this guy just happens to show up in Corden, at the Wilcox Hotel, in Lilybell's room, when the only guy he's talked with about this woman was Sigmund's old man. He doesn't know what it all means, and the kid's in no shape to tell him, so he hauls him down to his car and scat-asses out of town. But he figures at this stage he needs a doctor to bring the kid around, one who won't be nosing into how the kid got hurt, and he needs a place to hide out. So who does he think of but his old buddy and kissing cousin, Tiny Fox? I figure he called you, and you put the twos together and got a combination that made you call Doreen Cutter."

"Why in hell'd I do that?" He sounded as if he really wanted to know.

"Simple. Your family's never been exactly tickled pink with the way Wayne wound up with all the loot left by the colonel. So if you could convince Doreen that her hubby had pulled off a little stunt that might have got her son killed outright, it would sure as hell land him in big trouble if he had tried settling things with Hack for killing the widow. I figure you told Doreen you could fix her up with grounds for divorce that would leave her holding the family fortune, and make a deal for her to turn over a certain percentage of the business operations to Foxes that had it coming."

Tiny shook his broad head in wonder. "By God, you got imagination that won't quit."

"Uh-huh. But it hasn't been good enough for me to figure out the business with Murduff. Did he show up after Hack clobbered Sigmund? If he did, what was his angle? A little blackmail pitch based on stuff he got from me when I went around to question him? If that's it, how'd he know where to find Hack?"

"You've had all the answers so far, keep at it."

"Was Murduff's wife a Fox?"

"That's no crime."

"I'm beginning to think it should be. How about if she knew a likely place where you'd put up Hack, and spilled that to her hubby?"

"Okay, say she did. So what? Who cares about all that?"

"Cops have to put together a story that adds up. It'd help if we could hand them a nice straight answer to why Hack thought he had to kill him."

"Okay. He killed him 'cause the bastard tried shaking him down. What else do you need?"

"Will you admit to Ahern you helped Hack get a doctor for Sigmund and gave him a place to hide out?"

"I only offered help for a damaged guy and shelter for the pair. No hideout. You can't nail me for that. Besides, after two days they both took off—that was it."

"Look, I'm not one damned bit interested in putting your tit in a ringer. I just want Ahern to have a clear case against Wayne Cutter. It'll have to be ironclad, because the bastard has loot and connections."

Tiny folded his hammy arms across his massive chest and scowled a few seconds.

"Okay. Lemme talk with my lawyer. We'll see what he thinks. Meanwhile, you keep shut. You go blabbing, and I won't give you shit."

"How much time?"

"Come back in an hour."

"With bells on."

36

THE LAWYER WASN'T happy about me, but he sat in when I showed up back in Tiny's office. It was apparent that if he had his way, Tiny would have given me the heave-ho. But I'd figured my man right. Tiny wasn't the cautious type, and he was intent on giving Wayne Cutter all the trouble he could offer. We talked some more, and finally he agreed to meet with Ahern if I'd bring him around.

I filled Ahern in on the way, and he arrived at the Fox den in a highly cooperative mood. The cop and I went from Tiny's place to where Sigmund was hiding out.

Wayne was arrested that evening, taken downtown, booked, and parked in a cell for nearly an hour before his lawyer bailed him out.

I wish I could say Wayne was nailed as an accessory to murder, and Sigmund got off clean. It didn't turn out that simple. Their cases were tried separately. Sigmund was convicted, but because of mitigating circumstances, he got a light sentence, a lot of probation, and wound up pretty much of a local hero. I found it interesting that no one made any big deal about the weird timing involved in the death of Hack, nor did anyone question how come he survived over a week after the beating from Hack, without the services of a doctor or any sustenance, and still was capable of clobbering the muscle man in a hotel no one ever located.

Of course, for all we really know, Sigmund might have been covering for his little brother. What it really boils down to is, nobody gave a damn what happened to Hack and didn't worry about the details of his death.

When Wayne's trial came up, the jury, thanks to his lawyer, who was as good as you'd expect a son of the colonel's son to be, raised enough doubts in the jury's mind to keep them from coming through with a guilty charge. The judge lectured Wayne on irresponsibility and miserable judgment for a community leader and set him free.

He didn't come out that well in the divorce court. Doreen's lawyer was as sharp as Wayne's and Doreen was a hell of a lot better in the witness box than her husband. The judge wasn't subtle about his sympathy for her, and the settlement was enough to have broken a sensitive man. Of course, that wasn't one of Wayne's weaknesses. The last I heard, he was making out fine with a new, younger, and more manageable wife, but had a pretty limited social life.

Sigmund married Marlene and moved to Minneapolis. Gunnar went to the University of Iowa and majored in journalism.

Tiny Fox was cock of the walk with his clan, thanks to generous partnership arrangements with Doreen. His feet recovered from the damage suffered in his waltz with me, and he's moving around as well as can be expected for a man of his size and poundage. I've been told he leaves barroom bouncing to the younger generation of the family these days.

05-99

F   Adams, Harold
         The ice pick artist.

DEMCO